THE BOOK OF RONDALATION VOLUME 2

Table of Contents

ESCAPE TO HELL:
Stuck In Traffick

L. MA'SHELL

CHAPTER 1

I snuggled up like a content cat on my new Platform bed. I had a feeling it might be lower than I prefer, even though others would find it just right. To make it perfect, I decided to use two mattresses: a 10" memory foam mattress on the bottom and a 13" Purple Mattress (the brand, not the color, though it is actually purple and my favorite). With these mattresses, my platform bed now feels like a luxurious bed fit for a princess, albeit not as high as the Princess and the Pea story. Ever since getting this bed, I have been enjoying the most incredible nights of sleep!

Tossing and turning in bed, I recalled a melody stuck in my head from the night before, prompting me to get up and write it down with God's guidance. Despite my drowsiness, I followed His lead to capture the song's essence. Acknowledging His persistence, I started penning the lyrics, appreciating the musical talents He bestowed upon me, resulting in my recent album release, "Grace to Love."

In the midst of writing, I unintentionally fell asleep at my desk, only to be awakened by the discomfort of my head hitting the floor. I just laid there staring at the ceiling. "Ok Lord, with all due respect, you could've awakened me to go to bed just like you did to get me out of it!"

Reflecting on my journey with God and music, I readied myself for a studio session with my friend and producer, Ryan Scott. Our shared passion for music led us to create our first album, overcoming life's challenges. Now, we are focused on our new project, guided by God's purpose.

As I prepared for the session, I expressed gratitude to the Lord for His guidance and provision, embracing His plan for our musical journey. With a heart full of thanks, I set off with the assurance of God's presence leading the way.

CHAPTER 2

I entered the expansive studio with a wide smile, marveling at the purple accent lighting that Ryan had installed just for me. The hardwood floors glistened, reflecting like a mirror. The studio boasted top-of-the-line equipment and instruments. The main recording booth was spacious enough for an ensemble yet intimate for a solo singer. I felt proud of Ryan for venturing out and establishing his own recording studio, The Ryteway Recording Studio.

"And here I thought you were thrilled to see me!" Ryan greeted me warmly as he walked over for a friendly hug. "I'm always happy to see you. I'd be even happier if you got me that purple mic from Studio Central Magazine," I teased.

"You have your lights, don't push it!" he joked back. My name was elegantly displayed in purple cursive over my assigned vocal booth. Today marked my first recording session in it. These luxuries didn't come easily; Ryan and I worked hard, guided by faith, to create this masterpiece of a studio. While Ryan's creativity and skills were the backbone, he ensured my involvement not just for my contributions but also due to our close friendship. Though some mistake us as a couple due to our compatibility, our bond is too precious to risk. We shared immense respect for each other.

After our opening prayer, Ryan suggested we start with warm-ups.

"I did them before coming," I protested.

"Do them again so I can test the new sounds on my keyboard," Ryan insisted. I relented with a laugh. Ryan's childlike enthusiasm for music and equipment always amused me.

Entering the booth, I chuckled, realizing it was the temporary one. Unveiling the microphone, I was thrilled to see a two-toned purple and gold-trimmed mic. Ryan played a smooth jazz melody as I hummed into the mic, my voice enveloping the room. The acoustic warmth comforted me, and my voice flowed effortlessly, echoing God's love. Ryan's musical accompaniment blended seamlessly. I was so engrossed in the music that I didn't notice the speakers hidden in the wall. We recorded flawlessly, even adding background vocals without error, a rare feat for me.

As I exited the booth, I heard a slow sarcastic clapping. Is that even a thing? Well, if not, let's make it a thing now because the expression on this woman's face perfectly matched the clap.

"So Ryan, is this your new project for the concert competition? She has a beautiful voice, but why wouldn't she? She definitely has the weight to carry it off the way she did. Oh, no she didn't!

"Excuse me?" I replied, clenching my fists by my sides, reminding myself to stay calm. Isn't it just like the devil to interfere and cause trouble when he's upset that you're using your gift for the Lord?! Ryan hurried over to me and restrained my arms closer to my sides.

"Do you want me to show you what else I can handle with my strength?" I retorted.

"Um, Athena, could you please wait in the main studio room? Your session doesn't start for another 15 minutes," Ryan said, releasing my arms and gesturing her towards the main studio room.

This tall, impeccably beautiful woman with flawless brown skin named 'Athena' stared at me with piercing eyes, flicked her long curly auburn hair, huffed at me, winked at Ryan, and strutted away feeling pleased with herself.

"What was that about?" I asked Ryan, slamming my fists against my waist. Despite that woman's hurtful comment, I do have a waist. I have a lovely size 12 hourglass figure, just with an extra 15 minutes in the bottom glass. I look fantastic in my clothes, and I am confident in my own skin. She better hope I stay prayed up!

"And what's all this about the concert competition?" Ryan raised his hands, signaling me to give him a chance to explain.

"I was planning to discuss it with you later. Athena is a new recording artist and an old friend. She hired me to produce her next album. She's also participating in the competition with her brother, Aaron, as her musician. It's for musician and singer duos. I signed us up because I know we would excel!"

"And you didn't even think to ask me first?" I questioned. "The first prize is 50 grand! I know we could both use an extra 25 grand! I could pay off the remaining balance on the studio, and you could start on buying that theater you've been wanting!" He was right about that. I've been dreaming of opening a theater for live plays and community arts for a long time.

"Fine, but that doesn't excuse Athena's behavior!" I pronounced her name with a strong emphasis. "I don't know who she thinks she is, but I won't stand for it!"

"What happened to letting the Lord fight your battles?" Ryan remarked.

"I am His, and He is mine. He will us me to get 'er done!" Ryan threw his head back and chuckled.

"Girl, you know that's not right! Let's finish this session and pray afterwards because you seriously need it!"

"When is this competition and what are we going to prepare for it?"

"A few months away, and I'll go through all the details when I contact you later," he assured.

We wrapped up our session and said a prayer. As we bid goodbye with a hug, I noticed Athena glaring at us from the entrance of the main vocal booth. She stood with her arms crossed and wore a grin so sharp that I could see her lip crack. I stared back at her and said, "Goodbye Athena, it was a pleasure to not meet you!" then turned and left.

On the drive home, thoughts of Athena consumed me. What was her issue? Who was she really? I'll have Ryan send me a snippet of her recording so I can listen and see what I'm up against. Then, I had to reprimand myself for my attitude and thoughts, saying, "Lord, please fix me!"

Interrupting my thoughts, Ryan called to brief me on the competition held by The Chesterfield School of Music, a prestigious institution known for its scholarship fundraisers to support students' educational and artistic needs. This year marks their inaugural competition with a substantial prize. The school is renowned for discovering talent, attracting regular donations and sponsors, and giving back to the community.

As Ryan asked about my plans for the day, I spotted a dark figure by a neighboring bush. Although I couldn't see anyone after looking around, Ryan's voice broke my concentration. I assured him I was fine and heading home to practice songs for Praise & Worship, suggesting we collaborate on a competition piece. He agreed to come over.

Ending the call as I pulled my Alfa Romeo SUV in the driveway, I scanned the street, finding it deserted. My neighborhood in Chesterfield, Ohio, known for its cleanliness and friendliness, always made me appreciate God's presence in my life.

After securing my car into the garage, I noticed the garage back door was slightly open. Concerned, I grabbed my mace and a steel bat, thankful for the previous owners leaving it behind. Despite finding no one in the garage, I realized the intruder must be inside. Regretting leaving the kitchen door unlocked, I cautiously moved forward, ready to defend myself if needed.

I started strolling slowly from the kitchen into the dining area, where a double-level marble countertop with a double sink divided the two spaces. Moving further, I turned the corner into the living room. I have a dislike for cluttered spaces, so I kept only the essential seating in this room, which was satisfactory. Despite its simplicity, the decor added a touch of comfort, creating a relaxed atmosphere. Everything seemed in order, and there were no signs of disturbance or unusual noise, only the refrigerator doing its normal soft sing-song hum as any new refrigerator would do.

I strolled over to the bay window to double-check that it was securely locked, and it was. Moving through the living room, I headed towards the hallway with a bathroom nestled between two bedrooms. Passing by the sofa table positioned between the master bedroom and the bathroom, I quickly scanned it to ensure everything was in its rightful place. On the table, there's an 8x10 family portrait featuring my parents, my older brother who is two years my senior, and myself. I find myself missing him dearly; it has been over five years since we last spoke after he relocated to Florida. Among the photos, there are two 5x7 frames - one displaying just me and the other showcasing my brother alone. The table is also adorned with a couple of plants and a few figurines positioned between the pictures, all neatly arranged. Everything appeared undisturbed.

I entered my spacious master bedroom, glancing around before placing my purse on the bed momentarily. Rethinking its position, I headed towards the closet, gripping a spray bottle tightly. Slowly, I turned the handle and pushed the door open, revealing a walk-in closet adorned with shoes, clothes, and purses on every wall. Finding a spot for my purse, I proceeded to the attached bathroom, ensuring everything was in order. Returning to the hallway, I peeked into the adjacent bathroom before heading towards my practice/prayer room. Just as I approached it, a noise from the kitchen startled me, prompting a quick prayer for protection.

Still holding the mace and the bat, I stretched the mace out in front of me with my finger on the trigger. I followed against the wall back toward the kitchen. The door handle was trying to turn and I heard clicking in the lock. I reached in my pocket and grabbed my phone to call Ryan. Why isn't he here by now? This is the time he needs to be! Just as he answered the phone, the kitchen door swung open and I screamed, sprayed, and called on Jesus! Someone had come into my house!!

CHAPTER 3

I could hear Ryan's voice emanating from my phone, which lay on the floor. The individual who had entered my house was now writhing on the floor, shouting my name and questioning my actions. As I gazed at him, I caught a glimpse of his face. "Jax? Is it really you?"

My brother! My brother Jax had come home! Oh no, I sprayed him with the mace! Ryan had come bursting through the doorway with his fists raised ready to fight whomever or whatever caused the chaos. "Ryan, it's Jax!" I said. He looked closer at the figure on the floor holding his face and still rolling from side to side. He reached down and helped him up. I ran to the sink, grabbed a dish towel from the drawer, and ran it under cold water.

"We need to get him outside, quick! Do you have any milk?" Ryan shouted to me. "How can you drink a glass of milk at a time like this, Ryan?" "It's not for me, for Jax's eyes! Milk works better and faster than water!" "Oh!" I said and darted to the fridge and retrieved the carton of milk. I drenched the towel with it and went outside to meet them on the back patio. I placed the towel on Jax's face and he held it there.

We sat on the patio while Jax regained his sight. The sun was hidden behind the clouds allowing the late afternoon to be comfortable with a slight breeze. Now I understood why Ryan was insistent on getting him outside.

"Jax I am so sorry! I didn't know it was you! Why are you here? Why didn't you tell me you were coming? Wait, how did you get in?" Jax, short for Jackson Xavier, had gotten pretty buff since the last time I saw him. He looked really good. He has a strong jaw line, chiseled cheekbones, full lips, and deep-set eyes, well from what I could make out anyway. His hair nicely faded. His skin is smooth and light-brown with an even tone. Florida seems to be treating him real nice.

"I got in town about an hour ago. A buddy of mine was coming to town and I decided to tag along. I figured it was time to come home for a visit. Apparently I got mixed up when I got on your street because I had my buddy drop me off at what I thought was your house. When I saw your car come down the street, I hid because I wanted to surprise you. I saw what driveway you pulled into so I hurried and ran around the back of the houses. I had to jump a few fences to get to yours, but I made it to the back door just as you were opening the garage. I climbed that tree next to the door and watched you check the back yard." He started laughing before he continued. "Oh man you should've seen your face!"

"You think this is funny? You scared me! I thought someone was breaking in or something!" I yelled this at him hitting his arm with each word. He raised his arms and hands trying to block the blows. Ryan nodded his head in agreement, but still laughed about it. He stood up and walked away from the patio table still chuckling. "You're right Sis. I apologize. I didn't mean to scare you." He wrapped an arm around my shoulder and pulled me in for a hug.

We all went inside and sat at the kitchen table. "You still never told me how you got in the house, Jax." I said. "You don't remember making me a key when you got the house? You told me anytime I come back home I could stay here." "Oh yeah, I did. Well you've been gone for so long I forgot!" I said defensively. Ryan returned to the table with a cup of tea for me and two bottles of sodas for him and Jax. We sat and talked a little while longer.

"Joy we still have a little time to go over the songs. I think we should get to it before it gets late." said Ryan. He stood up and shook Jax's hand and welcomed him home then headed down the hallway to the music room. "Jax, help yourself to whatever you want. Your bedroom is right next to the bathroom. There are clean towels and wash cloths in the linen closet of the bathroom and plenty of soap, toothpaste and extra toothbrushes. We will be across the hall going over the music, but it shouldn't bother you since I had everything sound proofed." "Good looking out, sis." he said. I stood up to head to the music room when Jax said, "Joy, can you stop by my room before you go to bed?" he asked. I shook my head yes and went to join Ryan.

After about an hour and a half of practicing, Ryan left. I locked up the house and went to talk to my brother. "Jax?" I said, knocking on his bedroom door. He opened it and motioned me inside. "What's up?" I asked. "I would like to join you at church this week. It would be great to see Pastor and First Lady Spencer again." he said. "You would? They would be so excited to see you too!" Pastor Ronald and First Lady Malinda Spencer are devoted individuals who serve as pillars of the community. Celebrating a decade of marriage and nine years in ministry together, they collaborate with leaders from the Chesterfield Music School. Their mutual love and admiration shine brightly, reflecting their reverence for the community and congregation. First Lady Spencer has a special affinity for the Praise & Worship Team, having led it initially. Occasionally, she delivers a moving solo to set the tone for her husband's message. Her mastery of the organ is unparalleled, effortlessly guiding the congregation through inspiring musical moments. The harmonious atmosphere at Grace Temple Community Church is truly remarkable.

We chatted a bit longer until both of us couldn't stop yawning. "Well, big brother, I'm heading off to bed now. I'm exhausted."

"I'll just lay here and catch some Zs too, Sis." I got up, walked towards the door, and opened it to leave. Right before stepping out, I turned back to my brother and asked, "Have you told mom and dad you're here?"

"Not yet," he replied, lowering his head.

"Jax, you really should give them a call. They'll want to know you're here, no matter how you left."

"I understand, Sister. I'll call them tomorrow." I approached him, gave him a goodnight hug, and expressed my joy at his return home.

Later, in my room, after showering and getting comfortable in bed, I prayed, "Dear Lord, thank you for this day. Thank you for safely bringing Jax home, despite his attempt to send me to you before the Rapture. Please continue to guide his heart and mind towards forgiveness and acceptance. I love you dearly, Jesus. Amen."

CHAPTER 4

"Jackson? Jackson Xavier Yantz, I can't believe you're here!" We were welcomed by Elder Trevor Stanton in the church vestibule. Known as the pastor's right-hand man, any matters related to the pastor required Elder Stanton's approval unless you had a direct line to the pastor. After a warm, masculine hug between Jax and the Elder, I mentioned that I would save us a seat and then head to the prayer room for Praise & Worship preparation. Just as I was about to leave, I caught the Elder giving me a look of pure lust, which made my stomach churn, prompting me to roll my eyes at him. Despite his charm, financial stability, and effective management of the church's affairs, he was not someone I favored. He is known for using his influence and charisma to manipulate situations to his advantage, especially with women. Women would often admire his physical attributes and leadership skills, acknowledging his role in maintaining the church's esteemed reputation within the community.

"Oh he is fine!" "Mmhhmm! Look at those strong arms and legs and broad shoulders!" "Oh yes hunty! This is tall, dark, and handsome right at my fingertips", the women would say while gathered in a huddle watching him walk by.

"Sister Joy!" I cringed at his voice behind me trying to catch up to me.

"Yes Elder?" I said with delightful sarcasm.

"I just wanted to give you a proper greeting. We didn't get to connect when you came in with your brother." "Well as you know, I have to go prepare for Praise & Worship. Now, if you will excuse me."I said turning to walking away. "Wait a second. I've been meaning to talk to you about going to dinner with me. Maybe we could go after church this afternoon?" "Thank you Elder, but I am going to be spending the rest of the afternoon with my brother."

"Well maybe he could join us. I could get Sister McIntosh to join us. You know she's single. It could be a double date."

"Thank you for asking, Elder Stanton, but really, I'm good." I swiftly walked away before he could suggest another dinner date, knowing his intentions were more about showcasing me as arm candy rather than genuine interest. As I arrived at the prayer room door, I glanced back to see him with a charming grin and arms folded, gazing in my direction. A woman, whom I hadn't noticed earlier, had a disapproving look on her face - directed at him or me, I couldn't be certain. One thing's for sure, she doesn't need to worry about me.

Drake Landrow, the enthusiastic and histrionic praise and worship leader, approached the platform with us six team members positioned in a line behind him on stage, each with our individual microphones and stands. The team comprises 4 females and 2 males, with 2 voices assigned to each section of alto, soprano, and tenor. The harmonious blend of voices resonating from our mouths together is truly moving, with a focus on unity and balance.

Looking out at the eager audience in the sanctuary, I shifted my gaze to take in the beauty of the 500-seat venue. The plush burnt red carpet was complemented by the neatly arranged burnt orange cushioned seats in an auditorium-style layout. The walls were painted ivory with striking zigzag canvas paintings in burnt red, orange, and yellow adorning each one. Behind us, an ivory wall featured a Bible scripture painted in black, declaring, "Enter into His gates with thanksgiving, and into His courts with praise!" from Psalm 100:4-5. Carpeted stairs led up to the stage, adorned with large plants on each side, changing with the seasons. The band section was positioned on the right, while the protocol seating was on the left, offering a diagonal view of the platform and sanctuary.

"Come on everybody and stand to your feet! Let's show the Lord that we love Him and give Him praise on this morning! Hello? The Bible tells us that the rocks will cry out in our place! If you don't want the rocks to cry out in your place, give God a shout of praise! Come on! Think about all that He has done for you! All that He is doing for you! All that He is going to do for you! The fact that He gave His only son for you! That ought to make you want to run and dance in a shout of praise!"

Some followed Drake's instructions, while others sat, swaying to the lively music played by the band, anticipating the start of the first song. Silently, I prayed, "Father, in the melodious name of Jesus, please guide our Pastor as he delivers your message during this part of the service." Drake led the Praise & Worship session for three songs, delighted to see the congregation engaged and moving to the music. He then gestured for me to lead the final Worship song. The seamless transition was made easier by each of us having our own microphones. As the band smoothly transitioned into the next song, I closed my eyes, took a deep breath, and joined in worship by humming along with the music. I sang, allowing the Lord to take His rightful place.

> *There is no place like God.*
> *There is no place like God.*
> *There is no place, no place like God*

After I sang the first verse, I motioned for the team to follow in the same way, changing place to hope then to peace escalating each stance. After the last stance, we went into exhortation and worship to God. By this time the atmosphere had become thick with the anointing and presence of God! He is truly in the room! The entire sanctuary was shouting, praying, singing, and lifting their hands and faces towards the heavens! The band brought the vamp in with equal force and everyone joined in excitedly! The team and I allowed the Holy Spirit to have His way in us as we sang the parts and I adlibbed to direct the start of each line:

> *He is shelter in time of the storm!*
> *He will keep us safe in His arms!*
> *We stand in awe of all He can do!*
> *There is no place like God!*

The song ended on 'There is no place like God' abruptly with the echo of the team's voices lingering as if standing on a cliff and hearing them repeat off in a distance.

Pastor Spencer stood up, walked towards the podium, and motioned us to start back in with the vamp. I gradually began stepping towards my spot in line, but he touched my arm and directed me to stay where I was. He began to exhort and adlib some of the words himself, then nodded towards me to continue. He stepped down from the stage and looked to First Lady to join him on the floor. They began walking the floor back and forth in worship. They knelt at the altar in prayer. The congregation followed suit either at their seats or at the altar. I raised my hand to the band to direct them to play the song in a slower mode. I worshipped with 'There is no place, no place like God', adding a few other synonyms and melodic runs according to the atmosphere. The tears ran down my face slow and steady. I could not stop smiling at the presence God! As the team continued singing softly, I prayed and thanked Him for showing Himself strong in the building. I lifted my hands in surrender.

As the atmosphere became more peaceful, Pastor Spencer took the podium again and spoke to the congregation reminding them how God moves in and around us if we let Him. He continued on, preparing everyone for the word. We quietly exited left of the stage and down the steps to the prayer room door. I took a seat in one of the chairs in the corner of the room and buried my face in my hands. I had not come to myself yet. God was still dealing with my spirit.

I opened the door that led to the hallway off the sanctuary to exit the prayer room and there was Drake. He was blocking the doorway. "Can I talk to you for a minute?" he asked. I stepped back inside the room to take a seat. The prayer room is set up like a small choir room. It has 12 chairs, a podium, and a section for the musicians. The décor of the chairs and carpet are the same as the sanctuary.

Taking a seat next to me, Drake stares me in the face and says, "You are so amazing when you lead Praise & Worship."

"Trust me it's all God!"

"I know. That's what I admire about you. You always just go forth whether the people get with you or not. You just go in and do what you do."

"I strongly believe that the Praise Team is not here to get the people to feel God or be moved. That is something that they should already have done before getting here. I don't feel the need to tell them to do anything. If they allow themselves to become one with the Holy Spirit, He will tell them what to do."

"Listen, Joy, I've wanted to talk to you about something for a while. I think we work well together. I think we could make the Praise & Worship ministry grow even more together. I've been attracted to you since the first day I walked through the church's doors. I-"

"Whoa! Drake, I enjoy us working together and the friendship that we have, but that's it. I'm sorry. I am not interested in dating right now. People always seem to want that person that is so in tune with God because of how they function with Him outwardly, especially in the church. What they don't realize is what that person had to go through and what they have to continue to do to stay under that anointing. I have a lot going on with what God gave me to continue in ministry outside of the church building. There is no time or space for me to start dating right now."

"Well just remember you said "not right now" so I will check back with you again after a while."Drake said.

I stood up and patted his shoulder. "You did an amazing job today as well. Just remember, you don't have to play Simon Says to reach people."

He laughed and shook his head as I left the room.

Wow! I did not see that coming! Drake has never shown interest in me! I never even fathomed a relationship with him. We have always just worked all things Praise & Worship. Every now and then we would meet up for lunch or dinner, but even then it was music and song related in preparation for rehearsals and services. Drake is more of a people pleaser and attention seeker. That is just too much negative energy for me. I do, however, think he is very handsome. He is about 5' 8" tall with a shiny bald head, light-brown skin, and adorable facial features with dimples. He is husky and solid built, perfect cuddling material. Besides all of that, there were no mutual feelings on my end.

CHAPTER 5

"Okay, Athena, time to begin," Ryan said to Athena when I arrived at the studio for our Tuesday session. I moved to Ryan's desk, keeping my distance to avoid interrupting, and settled in to wait for my turn. Athena glanced at me, offering a sly grin, then took her place in front of the microphone, adjusting her headphones. Ryan noticed her glance at me, smiled, and nodded, to which I responded in kind.

"Let me know when you can hear yourself." Ryan said to her. She told him she could hear fine and that she was ready to start recording. He adjusted a few knobs and began the music. On cue, Athena sang her lyrics. Her voice flowed out melodic and enchanting. It possessed a rich and resonant tone, that effortlessly hit both high and low notes. She really could sing! Her voice really matched her beauty! I couldn't help but notice, though, that the passion wasn't as strong as the talent. Still, it was good enough for her to win the competition. She kept taking glances at me and grinning as if to say, "Yeah now what?" I just continued watching her. I was actually starting to feel sorry for her because it was like she felt she had something to prove. Allowing yourself to take on that type of responsibility takes away from who you really are and what you really should be doing. It also explains why her lyrics have nothing to do with The Lord or His purpose; especially since she is the praise and worship leader of her family's church;

according to Ryan. Either way, with that voice and those looks, she could really make it in the world.

When their session was over, I got up and began walking towards my own personal studio room. Athena did not hesitate to meet me halfway.

"Knowing what you're up against, I think it would be best if you just went ahead and dropped out of the competition now. Save you the embarrassment!" she said as she folded her arms and stood firm.

"You don't even know me. What is your problem?" I asked, not backing down from her.

"I know enough!" She dropped her arms to her side, gave me a scowled look, and then stormed off. I continued my path to the studio room. I looked through the glass and seen that Ryan had his headphones on. Apparently he had no idea what just took place. I decided not to say anything about it to him at that moment.

We finished our session. I exited the room and walked over to Ryan. "Please tell me what your girl's problem is! She approached me after the session telling me I should drop out of the competition and save myself the embarrassment!"

"She's very competitive, that's all."

"She doesn't know me to treat me the way she does!"

"She's intimidated by you."

"What for?"

"You're good and she knows it. Listen, Joy, you have a true gift. Athena has true talent. There's a difference. She's always been the competitive type. Whether it is about looks, academics, or especially music and singing, she has to come out on top. I will say, though, I have never seen her bent out of shape about anyone like she is about you."

"That's just crazy! Well, I am not going to let her get to me. I am going to continue on as God leads me!"

"As you should! See you at praise and worship rehearsal Friday?"

"You sure will!"

I pulled into my driveway next to an olive green SUV with tinted windows. Jax must have company over. I hope it's not a bunch of guys being loud making a mess in my house. I pulled further into the garage. When I stepped into the house, I didn't hear anything. "Jax?" I called out. "Jax, are you here?" No answer. I heard a muffled sound coming from his room. I hurried down the hallway to his door and grabbed the door handle. Just as I was about to swing it open, I heard a woman's voice, then Jax saying, "Girl, you keep moving like that and I will explode all over you!" I gasped and backed away from the door. I couldn't believe he had a woman here in my house having sex! Of all the disrespect! Anger welled up inside me and I went back to the door and banged on it. "Jackson Xavier Yantz, come out here right now!" After a few moments of shuffling and bumping around, he came to the door showing only his face.

"Sis, what are you doing here?"

"Being the owner and operator! What are you doing here?" I used my hands to gesture towards the bedroom acknowledging the awkwardness.

"I have company right now!"

"That's all fine and good, but I do not appreciate the kind of company you're having in my house, Jax! You know I don't roll like that and I am definitely not going to let anyone else roll like that in my house either! Why can't y'all go to her house?" Jax asked me to hold on for a minute while he got dressed.

I walked to the kitchen and sat at the table. A few moments later Jax came rushing in.

"Sis, I didn't mean to disrespect you or your house. It didn't even start out this way. We were just sitting and talking and then one thing led to another. I'll go ask her to leave, then we can sit and talk some more." I just sat staring at him as he talked. He got up and did as he said. Apparently he knew not to bring her in my face for an introduction. That or she was afraid to confront me because I heard the front door close and lock without hesitation.

"Some of the guys and I went out to eat earlier then went to the bowling alley. After bowling a few games I was ready to leave, but they weren't. I was going to call an Uber when Monique approached me. We got to talking and she offered to bring me home. She asked if she could use the bathroom when we got here. When she came out I offered her something to drink, I figured it was the least I could do since she brought me home and wouldn't take any gas money."

"Let me guess, she had a better way of repayment?" I piped in.

"Look, you know I used to really like her back then. I had no idea she'd look as fine as she did today! I really am sorry, Sis! It won't happen again, I promise!"

"Have you spoken to mom and dad yet?" He got up and went to the sink, reaching into the cabinet to take out a small plate. "I tried, Sis," he mentioned while lifting the lid off the cake plate, revealing the delicious leftover chocolate Bundt cake with cream cheese icing that I had prepared for us to have for dessert after a home-cooked Sunday meal. It consisted of tender baked lemon pepper chicken breasts in garlic butter, a medley of peas and carrots, mashed potatoes, and baked rolls. We were eagerly looking forward to returning from church to enjoy that feast.

Cutting into the half eaten cake he said, "I called them. Mom answered the phone. I talked to her for a little while and let her know I was here. She had me hold on while she went to get dad. When she laid the phone down, I hung up. I just couldn't do it. I could not bring myself to talk to him."

"Jax, you have got to talk to him. Forgiveness is a very powerful gesture. How long are you going to hold this over him? Look at how successful you've become in spite of what he did to you." He grabbed a fork from the drawer, leaned against the sink counter, and forked a piece of cake from his plate. Filling his mouth with it, he closed his eyes and said, "Mmmm mmm mmm! You straight put your foot in this cake my sista!"

"You already had about 4 slices since Sunday, dude! Stop acting brand new and talk to me!" I stood up and grabbed the plate and fork from him. I sat back down and slammed the plate on the table.

"Dang, girl! You didn't have to take my cake! Look, I haven't talked to dad in years. I've been so angry at him I didn't know how to talk to him. I was afraid that as soon as

I heard his voice, I would get angry all over again. I mean, what do you say to a parent, whom you've entrusted your entire life to only for them to rip away everything you've worked for on purpose for their own selfish reasons?"

"Jax, dad has been trying to make things right with you ever since that day. You could at least hear him out! I don't like what he did no more than you do. It was mean and underhanded for him to pretend to be you in turning down that scholarship."

"Joy, he didn't just pretend to be me, he hid my acceptance letter! You know how hard I worked to get that scholarship to Florida State! It was more than just football for me. There were other opportunities for me that would give me something to fall back on if football didn't work out! Luckily, those other opportunities came through for me in a huge way and I was still able to get in at Florida State under a different scholarship! What he did changed my respect for him!"

He's right. It was the principle of it all. Our father had been selfish all those years ago. Jax and I are products of PK's. As a pastor, our father made it a point to make sure his family and household followed the Bible to the letter when it came to upholding the church. We lived, ate, and breathed church six days a week. Saturdays were auxiliary days. Whatever auxiliary was having a function, we had to be there to support it. We weren't allowed to have friends that were not in the "church". The weekdays consisted of school, homework, dinner, church. And of course church all day Sunday-morning and evening service. Our father wanted Jax to take the seat in the pulpit next to him to be groomed for his role when he got older to keep our church in the family. But Jax wanted to play football. When he was in 8th grade, he made up excuses to stay after school so he could hang out in the field and play football with his buddies. Sometimes a few of their fathers would join them and give them pointers or just toss the ball around with them. Jax was so jealous of them in that way. He wished our father were more like them. He decided to ask our father to toss the football around with him hoping to share his heart's desire. Our father went into a sermon about how we were put on this earth to serve the Lord, not football. "No one is going to gain salvation through pig's skin!" he would say.

Jax tried out for the team in 9th grade and had somehow managed to hide practices and games from our father all the way through to his senior year. Since our father hardly watched television or read the newspaper, Jax knew it would be easy to keep it a secret. I hated that he always got out of going to church some nights, but at the same time I was happy for him. When the time came for him to start applying for colleges, he did it without our father's knowledge. Our mom, on the other hand, was more supportive and understanding about Jax's plans for football and college. She understood our father's motives and reasoning, however, she did not agree with how he went about them concerning us. But she knew how to handle our father in such a way that made him feel like he had made the final decisions in all matters when it was actually her who had the final say. She was very good at that.

A month after Jax relocated to Florida, we received news that our church had caught fire. The church had required substantial maintenance over the years, but the donations had not been sufficient to cover the costs. My father's income from working at the Plant was not enough to manage both the church repairs and support our household. Rumors circulated that our father had orchestrated the fire for insurance money, but these were dissolved when the investigation revealed years of faulty wiring. Jax interpreted the incident as a sign of God's wrath towards our father, so he decided not to return home during that period.

"Jax, please, just talk to him." I said.

"You know, you were always his favorite."

"Only because I sang in all the church's choirs growing up. Dad knew I was destined for ministry soon as I started holding vocal notes. He wasn't worried about me going anywhere." I chuckled thinking of how it was all a set up.

"Pray for me Sis. I know I need to talk to him, and I will. I just need a little more time."

CHAPTER 6

I have been working at my job for approximately six years. Today was unlike any other day I have ever encountered during my time there. It seemed like everything that could go wrong did go wrong. The electronic systems kept shutting down, restarting, and shutting down again at least five times throughout the day. Since our work heavily relies on technology, it made the day exceptionally difficult. If there was ever a day I was eagerly anticipating Friday, today was that day! I am genuinely excited for the Praise & Worship rehearsal this evening to unwind and let go of the stress from today!

Working for a Web Designing Firm is very tasking and yet very fulfilling. Bringing people's ideas and dreams to life on the screen to give their customer's the best experience of the products and services they have to offer them is something I take very seriously. I know what it's like to try finding the perfect web designer, which is why I decided to take classes and learn how to create them myself. The good designing companies are too expensive, and the affordable ones give poor service. The company I work for is teaching me to not just be good, but be the best in quality, service, and affordability. They were impressed with my knowledge and portfolio and decided to promote me to head designer on my team. I am now working towards going solo and starting my own web design business.

I decided to go straight to the church for rehearsal instead of stopping at home first. Rehearsal wasn't until

6:30 so I wanted to take advantage of the extra hour and a half of alone time in the sanctuary to reflect and allow the Holy Spirit to take control of my focus. I didn't have to worry about getting in this early because this was the second Friday of the month; the finance committee's meeting period. I pulled into the parking lot and cringed at the sight of Elder Trevor's Champagne Gold SUV parked in his assigned spot. I really hope I do not have to deal with him this evening. I pulled into a spot close to the door. When I stepped through the doors of the vestibule, there he was. I inwardly rolled my eyes. Expecting him to approach me, I prepared my mind to respectfully dismiss him. But he didn't. He looked surprised to see me come in as if I startled him or something. He had beads of sweat forming on his forehead. "Uh, sis-sister Joy, why are you here so early?" he stammered.

"I just wanted to have a few moments alone in the sanctuary before everyone showed up for rehearsal. Are you alright? You don't look so good."

"Oh I'm fine. Just came out for a little air. Needed a break from the meeting is all. Excuse me, I have to get back in there." he said, and hurried through the sanctuary and down the corridor to the finance office.

That was weird. Well, at least he didn't try to force his player status on me this time.

I entered the sanctuary, laid my purse on the front chair, and went to the altar. I knelt and began my communication with God. Once He rid me of the day's remnants, I began thanking Him in Worship. I allowed his presence to over take me. Just then, I felt a hand on my back and a praying voice. It was First Lady Spencer! She joined me in Worship!

When the Spirit lifted, she hugged me and said, "Joy, you have an amazing gift. I don't mean just your voice either. The way you intercede and go into Worship for others is truly God sent. Don't ever lose focus of what you have." She hugged me again and left the sanctuary. That meant so much coming from her. If anyone was in tune with God, she definitely was.

Ryan was the first to show up. We nodded at each other as he headed to the musicians corner to get set up. One by one the rest of the team entered the sanctuary. Drake was the last to arrive. He greeted everyone with, "God bless you all and thank you for coming out tonight." then proceeded to set up the sound room. After we tested the mics and warmed up the voices, we proceeded with rehearsal. Drake selected a soprano and a tenor to lead a song each. We made it through three of four songs. Before we started the fourth song, I needed to go to the bathroom. I excused myself and proceeded to do so. When I got to the ladies room the door was locked and a sign was on the door that said 'out of order'. Great, now I have to go to the one further down the corridor across the Pastor's office. Not that I minded, I just really needed to go and this meant that I would have to hold it longer. As I walked on towards the next bathroom, I noticed the door was slightly opened to the Pastor's study and the light was on. I decided to pop my head in and say a quick hello. Maybe I should go use the bathroom first. Nah, It will only take a second. I walked closer to the door and was about to knock when I saw something very strange going on. I looked a little closer through the crack in the door and gasped! "WHAT THE-!" I yelled involuntarily. I felt warm liquid gush down my legs. I guess you could say I decided to go to the bathroom first. I felt a hand from behind grab my face and cover my mouth and nose. Something strong smelling was quickly rushing up my nose making me light headed. I struggled to get away and to stop inhaling the smell. What is happening to me? Why did I just see-?

~~~~~~

Oh my head! I found myself lying on an old stiff couch. Where the heck am I? I stilled to see if I could hear any voices or noises or something to reveal my location. I grabbed my head and slowly sat up. It felt like someone had dropped an anvil on it. I forced myself to stand. I looked around trying to figure out where I was. Suddenly, I heard muffled voices. I looked around for the door. No door? How could there be a room without a door?? "Joy?"

Drake! That's Drake's voice! "Drake? Drake, I'm in here! I can't get out!" I heard knocking then Drake called my name again.

"Joy, are you ok? Where are you?" He must've noticed I wasn't in the bathroom.

I banged on all the walls in this small room. Where is the door!?

"Drake! I'm in here!" I stopped to listen for Drake. I think he's gone. Well apparently I'm still at church. But where? I remember standing outside the Pastor's door
~~~~~~

before I was knocked out with chloroform. Really? Chloroform? Who does that? I felt along the walls again looking for a door or a window. The room was the same size as the prayer room bathroom; small but able to snugly fit two narrow stalls with toilets and 1 small sink. There were none of those in here. It was poorly lit so all I could make out as far as décor was orange and red floral carpeting, the three seat orange couch that I woke up on, and paneling covering the four walls. The smell was slightly familiar, not bad or good, I just couldn't think of where I smelled it from.

My phone! My purse! Where were my things! I left them on the front row in the sanctuary! I have got to get out of here! "Hello?!" I yelled. "Is anybody out there? I'm stuck in here! Somebody help me please!"

I heard a creaking sound behind me. I whirled around and saw a dark figure dressed in all black from head to toe; a skin tight mask, turtle neck top, black slacks and skin tight rubber gloves.

"Who are you? Where did you come from?"

"Quiet!" the deep voice belted out. I didn't recognize the voice.

"Who are you? What do you want?" I asked.

"I want you to shut up!" he demanded, then slapped me so hard I landed on the floor. When I tried to get up he grabbed my arm and yanked me up himself. He pulled me close to him and put his lips to my ear.

"You are going to do what I tell you to do without saying a word!"

I was holding my breath out of fear but also to refrain from smelling his bad breath. He started rubbing my back up and down with his gloved hands.

I gasped in surprise. His hands moved further down to my behind and he lowered his head to my neck.

"Ooh the things I would like to do to you." he said

"Please, let me go! I won't tell anyone about this!"

He tightened his grip on me. I could hardly breathe now.

"The only thing I'm going to let you do is introduce those pretty little lips to my special friend!" he said this while touching a finger to my lips then grabbing my hand and placing it on his penis. I yanked it away. He grabbed the back of my head and yanked it back by my hair. Now I was angry. My adrenaline kicked in. I grabbed his penis and squeezed, digging my nails in as hard as I could. I stomped my foot hard on top of his, then reared my knee back and replaced my hand with it-hard! He fell to the ground rolling in a fetal position and cursing me something awful. I found a large book on a small table next to the couch. I picked it up and brought it down on top of his head with all the strength I could muster. He stopped moving. I didn't care if he was dead. I hurried to the direction he came from. I pushed hard against the wall thinking there must be a hidden panel over here. On my third push, the wall moved forward on the right side. I pushed further to go through, and ran right into another guy wearing the same get up as the first. "Where do you think you're going?" he said angrily. "I knew I should've come in here the first time. Stupid fool!" he said this to the figure lying on the floor starting to come to. To me he said, "Good night my little songbird." Then he covered my face with the chloroform cloth again.

CHAPTER 7

Ok, they really need to knock it off with the chloroform! I woke up in a spacious and luxurious hotel suite, surrounded by elegant Victorian furniture with gold accents. As I looked around, I noticed a beautiful floral arrangement, a marble dining table with high back chairs, and a large screen TV mounted on the wall. It felt surreal to see the room's opulence. Getting out of bed, I realized I was dressed in black sweats and a perfectly fitting black v-neck t-shirt. Confusion set in as I wondered who orchestrated all of this and where my own clothes were. Thankfully, I didn't feel any discomfort in sensitive areas, so I knew I hadn't been harmed. As I searched for a phone, I glanced out the window only to find a high balcony wall blocking the view. It puzzled me why there was patio furniture if the view was obstructed. Attempting to open the door, I discovered it was locked, leaving me with more questions than answers.

"You may as well get comfy honey, you ain't goin' nowhere!" a tall beautiful woman was sitting in the high back dining chair wearing lingerie. Where did she come from? I thought I was alone in here. I backed away from the door and bumped into the sofa table. I hugged my back to it and grabbed the edge to steady myself.

"Who are you? What is this place?" I asked, my voice shaking. As she was about to speak, the door swung open, revealing a stranger gesturing for me to follow him. I hesitated.

"Listen, dear, you'll soon realize it's best to follow instructions around here!" the woman remarked. She glanced at the man and added, smirking, "Where are you taking her? She's the ideal candidate for this role!"

Ignoring her, the man seized my arm and led me out of the room. I wanted to resist and protest, but the fear of being drugged again held me back. I was determined to uncover the truth behind my situation and the reason for it.

We proceeded to the end of the hotel corridor and entered a smaller, dimly lit room. Through a solitary window, I caught sight of a brick wall. The faint light revealed the room's gray, thin carpet. As the man pushed me inside, my feet confirmed the carpet's texture. Wait, where were my shoes? Only now did I realize I was barefoot. The plush carpet in the previous room had masked this fact. Walking barefoot irked me! Couldn't they have left my socks on at least? Sheesh! The room contained a full-size bed and two square wooden tables in the center, each surrounded by four uncushioned chairs of identical design.

The medium height emotionless man dressed in a black suit and tie over a white shirt pulled out one of the chairs and forced me to sit down. A crackling static sound came from inside his suit jacket. He reached in and pulled out a walkie talkie.

"Yes?" he answered.

"Do you have her?" a deep distorted voice responded.

"Yes."

"Make sure she ends up in the right place this time. I can't believe the incompetence I'm dealing with!" said the voice angrily.

"Will do." he said dryly. He placed the walkie talkie back inside his jacket and left the room.

"Wait! Where are you going? Why am I here?" I shouted after him but he ignored me and shut the door behind him.

I walked over to the window in hopes of seeing where I was, but the brick wall was too high and too wide. I couldn't even tell where it began. I walked over and sat on the bed. I consider myself a strong willed resilient person. Not afraid of anything besides missing the rapture, of course. I had no intentions of doing that. Right now, I am scared, alone, and confused. "Lord you are my refuge and strength. A very present help in the time of trouble. Take over the fear and confusion. Help me hear from you through all of this." I prayed and cried. I thought about Jax, my parents, and Ryan. I wondered if they were looking for me. They had to be. I missed them so much. "Lord please let them find me." I laid down curled up in a fetal position.

Sounds of scraping and scratching caused me to jump awake. I hadn't even realized I fell asleep. I sat up. My heart started pounding so loud I could hear it in my ears. I looked around the room but didn't see anything. The noise started again. It was coming from the bottom corner of the wall by the window. There was a vent there. I stared at it wondering what size rat was about to squeeze through it. I pulled my legs up on the bed and scooted back against the headboard. The screws from the vent started popping out one by one at each corner. I was breathing hard and shaking, looking around for a weapon. I got up, grabbed one of the chairs, and held it high over my head. The vent popped away from the wall. I gasped and pulled the chair over my head. This must be some rat even though the vent was spacious enough for a small person to pass through, or possibly for a small hunched adult. An adult? Oh no, not another kidnapper! But why would they come through the vent? Aren't they all working together in this whole thing? Or do they have an arch nemesis that feels they could do better in taking me off their hands? The thing that emerged from the vent left me speechless. I couldn't believe my eyes!

"Athena?" I lowered the chair and put it back in its place under the table. "What are you doing here? How are you here and why are you coming out of the vent?" I stopped for a moment and thought about what was happening. "Girl, if you are behind all of this you can best believe I am about to give you the beat down of your life!"

"Oh pipe down and listen mighty mouse! We need to get you out of here!"

"You came to rescue me? How did you even know I was here?"

"I have been following you around since I found out who you were."

"What? Who am I?"

"I will explain everything once we are out of here. Right now we have got to move!"

She grabbed my hand and pushed me toward the vent.

"Get in! Go!"

"How do I know I can trust you?"

"You don't know! What other choice do you have? Do you want to stick around here and find out what they got next for you? Now go!"

"You go first because I have no clue where I'm going!"

"Fine! You have to crawl as quiet as possible! We can still be heard in here!" she scoffed and led the way.

I followed her through the vent space keeping up with her pace as quiet as possible.

"How much longer until we escape from this place?" I whispered.

"Be quiet! Just come on!"

I sighed and continued on. Finally, I felt a breeze and figured we had to be close to an outside opening.

"This way!" she said, and veered to the right of the vent space which indeed led us to an outside opening. The area did not look familiar to me at all. It looked deserted. I was very relieved that it was still daylight

"Where are we?" I asked.

"I don't know, I think I made a wrong turn in there. But, hey, at least we're out of there! Come on, let's find a street sign!"

"Look, I am overly grateful that you found me. I still want to know why you've been following me."

"Joy, I promise, as soon as we get further away from here, I will tell you all about it."

I sighed. "You'd better. Let's go!"

CHAPTER 8

Athena and I walked through the streets of nowhere just as lost as when we first escaped from the vent.

"Now that we are further away from the building I can turn my phone on."

"Praise Jesus! You have your phone! Please let me call my brother!" I said excitedly.

"Well, Joy, I would if I was getting a signal out here" she said as she held the phone up in the air waiting for the towers to notice it.

"Of course! Of course we wouldn't have a signal out here! This is the typical horror story! It will be dark soon and we are out here in the middle of Michael and Jason's backyard!" I said in frustration.

"Stop being dramatic already! Besides my battery is low from it trying to connect anyway!" she said.

"Listen, Athena, I need you to tell me what's going on right here, right now!" I grabbed her shoulders to face me. She stared at me with an angry look. Then her face softened and her eyes watered.

"Joy, do you remember what you saw in the Pastor's office that night?"

"What?" I asked shocked that she knew what I couldn't remember. "How do you even-oh, right, you followed me. After being forced to inhale chloroform twice, I had a hard time remembering anything after walking to the bathroom. It wasn't until you came through the vent that everything came flooding back to my mind." She turned and began walking again. I stepped in line with her staring in her face for an answer.

"Well, after you went inside the church I managed to slip in without being seen. I hid in the cloak room to wait until rehearsal was over so I could continue my pursuit."

"Stalk much?" I said sarcastically.

"Just listen please!" I held up my hands to urge her to go on. "Shortly after I saw you take the corridor, someone suspicious looking sneakily stepped out of one of the class rooms and walked in the same direction behind you. I checked my surroundings and found an alternate way to that corridor without being seen. I grabbed an umbrella from the holder and carefully followed behind. I couldn't believe how clueless you were to everything except that slightly opened door with the light shining through it."

That remark made me feel some type of way. Was she mocking me?

I gave her a 'watch it' look.

"Anyway, when you went to the door and saw whatever it was you saw, he reached around you and covered your face with the cloth. I hit him with the umbrella, but it didn't affect him at all. He then turned and punched me. I went out like a light."

"I can't believe you came to help me and ended up getting got! As much as I want to return the mocking favor, I won't. I really appreciate you doing that." She just looked at me then continued.

"When I came to, I was in the same room you were in. You were still out. I tried to wake you. I even tried to lift you up to make you stand but you were dead weight and

I couldn't. This guy came out of the wall, grabbed me and chloroformed my face. When I woke up I was in the back of a van. There was a guy with a gun watching me. All I could see was his eyes. He wore a mask that covered the rest of his face. He had on all black and wore black leather gloves. I looked downward avoiding his gaze and that's when I saw you laying there. I snapped my head back up at him and asked him who he was and what he wanted. He just laughed at me."

"Wow!" I exclaimed. "I was probably on my second dose of chloroform by then. When I came to in that room, I heard Drake calling my name. I was calling back to him, but he couldn't hear me. A masked guy dressed in black came out of the wall and tried to-"I stopped and cringed at the thought of almost being forced to do something unethical to him. "Let's just say he wanted to introduce me to his little friend he had tucked away in his pants. When I dismantled him and his friend, I tried to go out the way he came in, but ended up running right into one of his buddies. And just like that, I was out like a light again." Athena wrinkled her nose, getting the hint of what I was almost made to do. She shook her head and continued her story.

"When the van stopped, I thought I was going to be drugged again or at least blindfolded or something, but he just motioned the gun at me to get out. There was no chance of running because as soon as the door opened there were four more goons standing there. Two of them grabbed me and the other two stepped in and got you. One of them threw you over their shoulder like a sack of potatoes. He was rubbing his face along your backside. I yelled at him to stop and the goon that contained my arms slapped me and told me to shut up. They were talking about putting us in the same room and having their way with us and laughing about it. The one that had the gun told them to shut up and that wasn't the reason we were there. We were in the back of a building walking through a door next to the dumpsters. At first I thought they were going to throw you in one but they didn't. I paid close attention to our surroundings looking for a way out. We walked a few feet down a long hallway stopping at a door with the number three on it. They opened the door, pushed me inside, and followed right behind me. The guy that had you thrown over his shoulder plopped you down on the bed copping feels along the way. I was furious! They locked me in a closet after I went off on them. After about 15 minutes they opened the door and let me out. I noticed they changed your clothes, which for that I was thankful because you reeked of pee."

"Oh yeah, I did wet myself when I saw-" I stopped talking. "Sorry, go ahead and finish."

Before she continued she looked at me like she was debating on asking me what I saw.

"You wet yourself more than just one time, honey! Anyway, I told them I had to use the bathroom. While I was in there I heard them leave the room. I also heard their footsteps through the vent that was on the wall close to the floor next to the toilet. The cover of the vent was flimsy, but couldn't be removed without releasing the small screws from the four corners. I bent down to look through the pattern of squares. The space between the vent and toilet as well as the space inside of it were just big and wide enough for me to crawl through. I thought about how it would work for you since you have bigger hips than I do. No offense, just stating the facts." She hurried to cover herself when she saw the threat on my face.

"Anyway, I saw their footsteps walking in the same direction we came in, going towards the end of the hallway. I took a bobby pin out of my hair and scraped the waxed tip off. It fit perfectly in the screws of the vent so I unscrewed them and lifted it from the wall. I went to the door to hear if there was anyone in the room besides you. I quietly opened it a little and saw you were still lying on the bed and everyone had gone. I came out and tried waking you up again, but to no avail. I heard footsteps coming back to the door so I ran back into the bathroom. I heard a woman's voice say, 'Yeah, I'll sit here with her.' That made me think she didn't even know I was there. They must've forgotten about me. Shortly after that I heard the door open again and a guy said, 'come with me' then the woman said something like, 'you'll learn to do as you're told around here, honey '. That let me know you were finally awake. I went back to the vent and saw two sets of feet walking in the same direction the other guys went-yours and I'm sure the guy who told you to go with him. I hurried through the vent listening closely to follow the footsteps. I didn't anticipate a turn and got nervous that I was lost, but I kept going until I saw a light coming in view. When I reached where it led, I looked through and there you were curled up on a bed."

"I can't believe you cared enough not to leave me there. I seriously thought you hated me for some reason. Thank you, Athena, seriously." I hugged her close. When I let go she was staring out behind me crying.

"What is it?" I asked.

"Look where we are!"

I turned away from her and looked in the direction she was looking. We were standing on a back road that had the church's view in sight. It was quite a distance away, but there it was nonetheless. I hadn't realized we even walked this far. Now I'm wondering how far was far between the distance of the church and that place! I kept the thought to myself.

"How are we going to get over there? It's nothing but cornfield all the way across." I said.

Looking up and down each road Athena pointed to the right at another dirt road and said, "There! We can go back down this road and be able to turn left to get to that one!" she said.

We trudged on with a more hopeful purpose this time. I couldn't wait to see Jax and Ryan. Most of all I couldn't wait to be HOME.

CHAPTER 9

Just as we turn the corner of the road leading to the church, a silver 2024 Lincoln Lithia drives up on us and slows down. "Run!" Athena says, and pushes me into the corn stalks. With the sun going down, it looks dark as we enter. We run far enough into it not to be seen by the person in the car, but we could still see them. The car stops in front of where we ran. A man with dripping Jheri Curls steps out and walks towards the stalks.

"Joy! Is that you?" He yells. I stare out at the tall lanky dark skinned figure dressed in a paisley rust and white button down shirt with orange slacks held up by a white belt with a large square buckle, and wearing white dress shoes.

"It's Deacon Kelso!" I tell Athena, rushing through the field to greet him. She follows close behind.

"Deacon Kelso! I am so glad to see you!"

"We have been looking all over for you! Are you ok? You've been gone for days! Your brother is worried sick!" Deacon says excitedly. He stretches out his lanky arms to greet me. I can smell his cologne before I even reach him. Deacon Roger Kelso is the head deacon of the church. He doesn't just help keep the church in order he also heads the security team for Sunday services. He dresses in a way that reminds me of someone straight out of the 70s.

I wrap my arms around is small waist in thankfulness.

"Come on ladies get in the car, I'll drive y'all to your house Joy. You'll both have to sit in the back because I'm having issues with the passenger side door for now."

We slide into the backseat of his luxurious car that smelled like leather and old spice. I slid in first sitting behind the Deacon, Athena slides in after me. It's hard to believe there are any problems with this beauty. I am in such anticipation of a long hot bubble bath that I could care less about his car's problems. I can't decide if I want to eat first or just slip into my comfortable bed wearing my purple cotton pj's after my bath.

"How did you know where to find us? Can we use your phone?" Athena asks.

"I didn't," he says, "I was on my way to the church to take care of some things and I saw you ladies walking."

"Athena, Deacon Kelso doesn't own a cell phone." I pipe in after he answers her first question.

"What? Who doesn't own a cell phone these days?" she asks.

"So where did you come from? Where have you been?" asks the Deacon. Athena and I tell the Deacon about our individual kidnappings and how we escaped. As he goes through the sympathetic and excitement responses, I look out the window longing to see my neighborhood come into view. I noticed we have passed the highway that leads to my side of town. I shrug it off at first thinking he is taking a different way, but then I notice something in my peripheral vision on the bottom right, hanging between the passenger seat and the middle console. My eyes widen. I secretly signal to Athena and point in the direction of the object. She looks and sees the same thing I see. Right there, in our plain sight, is a black full face mask! You could see where the eyes were cut out! The exact same mask worn by the kidnappers! Is

Deacon Kelso involved in all of this? Is he the one that drugged me? Athena pretends to have an itch on her foot so she bends down to 'scratch' it and feels under the seat in front of her. She pulls out a pair of black gloves and a white cloth with smeared lipstick. She pointed out silently that the lipstick was from her lips! Had to be from her because I wore lip gloss—no color!

The Deacon is still rambling. I interrupt. "Um Deacon, you passed the highway to my house back there. Did you forget where I live?" He came by a couple of time with Pastor and First Lady Spencer; once to bless my home when I purchased it, and again to pick up some items I was donating for our community give away at the church. Of course he didn't forget! He has a different agenda for us apparently! He ignored me and continued rambling. A few seconds later he just burst into laughter! What in the flim flam is happening in this car? I want to go home! The sound of a ringing phone came from the front seat. Athena gasped and looked over at me.

"I thought you said he didn't own a cell phone!"

"He made it clear last year that he didn't!"

He answered the phone still laughing. He didn't even say hello.

"Ah yes Sir, they are right here in the car with me. We are headed your way now." He hangs up the phone and looks at us through his rearview mirror. "Sorry my dears, I can't let you go now!"

"Where are you taking us?" Athena asked angrily.

"You'll find out soon enough." He said looking at us through the mirror again with a big cheesy grin on his face.

We continue driving down the dirt road for what seemed like forever until we pull over into a vacant lot.

"What is this place?" Athena says, and looks over at me with fear and confusion in her eyes.

"I know about as much as you do." I said staring out at the empty space from Athena's side of the window. Just then, a space in the ground slid open simultaneously from right to left about 5 feet to the right, in the same spot I stared out at. I mean it literally opened up! We looked at each other with our mouths hanging open.

"What in the world!?" we both say at the same time.

A white staircase with spaces in between each step rises from the hole, and Athena and I grab a hold of each other for dear life but not taking our eyes off of what was unfolding in front of us. Four men wearing black sunglasses and dressed in dark gray suits with black shirts and gray ties walked up the staircase once it finished rising. My heart thudded in my chest, and from what I could tell so did Athena's.

CHAPTER 10

Once the four men have ascended the staircase, they align themselves alongside the car on Athena's side staring over the roof of it with their hands behind their backs and standing at attention. They wore white ear pieces with coil cords draped behind their heads. I break my gaze from the four men and look in the front seat at Deacon Kelso. He's sitting there grinning from ear to ear watching in amazement as if looking at a movie screen.

"Who are these people?" I demand. "What are you going to do to us?"

"My job was to get you here. That's all I'm going to tell you." he said. Then he stepped out of the car and walked around to our door. Opening it he said in a GPS recording voice, "You have reached your destination. Please step out of the vehicle." He threw his head back and burst out laughing. Athena tried standing her ground and having us stay in the car, but when we didn't respond immediately, the Deacon grabbed us both by our arms and pulled us out. Who knew this lanky dude would have so much strength? He reminded me so much of a taller and black version of Squiggy from the classic TV show Laverne and Shirley. The 4 men opened the middle section of their stance to form an opening between them. Another man was coming out of the staircase! He also wore black sunglasses but he was dressed in a black suit with a gray shirt and black tie. He stands in front of us with no emotion and says, "This way!" and motions for us to follow him down the staircase. The 4 men are close behind us making sure we move forward.

Athena and I grab hands before we walk down the stairs together, both of us shaking like crazy! She leans her head over to me, not taking her eyes from facing front and whispers, "What do you think is down there?"

"How should I know?" I say. "I'm wondering what they are going to do to us once we're down there! I've already been pushed up on once and I definitely don't want it to happen again! There's more than one this time too!"

"I think if they were going to take us in that way, they would be rougher with us right now! They aren't physically forcing us or anything!"

"No but intimidation is forceful enough for me!"

We reach the bottom of the stairs to find a huge control room to the right of us. It's like an underground spaceship or something. Large flat screens are hanging on the walls all around us displaying radars and maps. There were beeps and radio sounds throughout. We just stood there in amazement, both of our mouths hanging open more confused now than before. The leader of the group notices that we've stopped walking and said, "Please follow me." and proceeded to lead us to a door in the back area. I grabbed Athena's arm.

"Oh no! I do not want to be locked up in a room again!" I said, and began to turn to run away. But I'm quickly reminded of the 4 men that are standing behind us.

"Joy, just chill out! It's not like we can do anything about it now! Let's just calm down! Besides, he said please!" Athena told me.

"What? How can you say that?" I asked in amazement at how she became so at ease all of a sudden. This time she grabbed me by my shoulders, stared me in the eyes and said,

"Panicking isn't helping! Think about it, at what point and time did any of the thugs say please or anything nice to us? None of these men manhandled us or spoke nasty to us!" She was right. The Deacon was the only one that had pretty much used force on us.

The man knocked on the door twice. The door opened and I squeezed Athena's hand a little tighter. A wave of astonishment swept over me like a huge beach tide, and I almost lose my balance at the sight of the man standing in front of us!

"Jax?" I managed to choke out in a rushed whisper.

"You know this man?" Athena asked.

I ran to him and threw my arms around him. I couldn't believe he was here! But wait, why was he here? How was he here?

"Jax, what are you doing here? Did you get captured too? Who are these people and why are they doing this to us?" The questions just kept shooting out of my mouth like I was at a gun range.

"You know this guy?" Athena asked, this time laying her hand on my shoulder and slightly yanking me to face her.

"Oh sorry, Athena. This is my brother, Jax. Jax, this is Athena."

"Athena?" he asked. "The one that gave you disrespect at the studio?" Athena looked at me then at Jax and said, "Yeah, I was trippin' that day."

I looked at her and said, "That day and every day we crossed paths."

The man that led us to Jax stuck his head in the room and said, "Sir, we need you to take a look at something on the radar."

Seeing that my brother was the only "sir" besides this man in the room, I said, "Sir? Why is he calling you sir like you're his boss or something? Jax, what exactly is going on here? What is this place and why are you in it?" He stood up, patted my shoulder, and left the room. Athena and I hurried after him.

I noticed that the four men that so happily greeted us upon arrival were each stationed at their own control section. They had taken off their suit jackets and were wearing short sleeved white button down shirts. Each one wore some type of badge or emblem on their left chest pocket. What in the crimeny is happening here!

CHAPTER 11

"We found movement over on the south side, Sir." said one of the officers pointing at the screen over his control section.

"Thank you, Fred." Jax said then proceeded to take a closer look at the screen. He gave instructions to the men then had Athena and I follow him back to the room. Judging by the name on the desk I knew we were in Jax's office. There is a large wooden desk and leather chair placed in the center of the room that sat on top of a large brown leather-lined area rug. Two more wooden chairs were placed in front of the desk for guests. The walls were adorned with large maps and white boards, and there is a movie screen hanging from the ceiling in front of one of the mapped walls. In the corner to the left of the door are two metal filing cabinets with six sliding drawers. The office looked like a classroom without the student desks.

"Ok, here's the deal." Jax began after closing the door behind us. "Joy, I am an FBI agent. I have been since I left home. Right now I am on a money laundering case. When we found out that the operation was housed here in Chesterfield, we informed our underground team and instructed them to find out their location and keep them under surveillance. I was assigned to this case because, of course, it's my hometown and who knows this place better than I do?"

"So that's why I hadn't heard from you all these years! And you're not here for a visit! Does mom know?"

"Of course not, but I will tell her before I leave."

"What about Dad?"

He gave me a knowing look and said, "Don't push it, Joy."

"Excuse me!" interrupted Athena, "not to break up your little reunion here, but what does all of this have to do with us? Why were we kidnapped?"

"I'm not really sure. I have a few of our guys working on the inside of their ring. They informed me that my sister was taken from the church."

"What? When? Which guys?" I asked, trying to think if I noticed a difference in man handlers.

"It was the second guy that entered the small room out of the wall. He pretended to be one of them to get you out of there. From what I understand, you handled yourself pretty well back there." I shivered from the reminder of that man's breath on my neck.

"Why didn't you all catch them?" Athena asked.

"Oh, we did. They are in custody now." Jax said.

"Did they tell you who their leader was?" I asked

"Of course not. The way their life is set up, it's better for them to be in jail with their tongues intact." He said. "We were also the ones that put you in that hotel that the both of you managed to escaped from." He leaned against the desk and folded his arms staring at us with a snicker on his face. Athena and I looked at each other and shrugged.

"So what happens next? Can we please go home now?" I asked.

"It's not safe for you to go home now, Joy. You ladies escaped from some dangerous people and you know too much for their taste."

"Wait a minute," Athena held up a finger for thought. "You mean to tell me that the men in the truck were your guys? Why would one of them feel Joy up the way they did and treat her like some cheap floozy?"

"Not all of the guys in the truck were with us. They had to play the part to get on the inside. They are still playing the part to help bust the operation."

"So is that Deacon guy with you too?" Athena asked.

"He sure is."

"Then that explains the mask and gloves we saw in his car." I said.

"Which means he was the one that drugged me!" said Athena.

"Yep, since you were in the way he had to play the role. He made sure not to dose you too heavy." Jax explained.

"So, what about my brother, how will I let him know I'm ok?" Athena asked.

"That's the thing. Until we shut down this operation, you two are going to have to stay here. No one can know where you are. As far as they're concerned, you're still missing. There's a search going on for both of you. I'm sorry Athena; this is also the best way to ensure your brother's safety." A sad look came over her face at this realization.

"Joy, the house is taken care of and still intact to your OCD liking. Now come with me and I'll show you where you'll be staying."

"Jax, what about Ryan? Did you at least tell him? He'll be worried sick." I asked. "I'm sorry, Sis, he still believes you're missing as well. We just can't take any risks."

Jax rose up from his leaning stance on the desk and walked over to one of the white board walls. He lifted the lid of a small white panel box that displayed push button dials and typed in a code. The white board slid open to the left and our mouths dropped. There is a huge room equipped with an eight seat movie theatre, an arcade section with the best arcade games including skee-ball, my favorite, and a full size kitchen! Jax led us to a set of double doors. "This is my favorite room!" He slid open the doors one at a time to reveal the most beautiful two story library that I have ever seen! The walls were cherry wood shelves filled with books from top to bottom and side to side! The ceiling was open in a rounded structure revealing a second floor. Spiral staircases were set on each side of the circle, wrapping it in their wooden open-step beauty! In the middle of the floor directly underneath the open ceiling, was an oversized round cherry wood reading nook complete with a built in cushioned bench and six soft red, yellow, and green throw pillows. The entire area has wall to wall carpeting with multi-colored squares. This place is unbelievable!

"It looks like this is going to be my favorite room as well, Jax! I said when I finally stopped ogling.

"Come on ladies, let's get you settled in and then you can come back out and play until your heart's content." Jax said, laughing at our amazement.

Just off the theatre was a hallway that had several doors, all aligned on each side of the wall like a hotel. Two more were at the end of the hall next to each other. Jax led us to those. He opened the door to the room on the right and then opened the door to the room on the left. "Joy, you're over here on the right and Athena, you're on the left." he said. I asked him who the other rooms were for besides him and the other five men. He explained they have a full kitchen and entertainment room staff that live onsite.

"What do we do for clothes? " I asked.

"Joy, you'll see that you have most of your things in there that I brought from home. Athena, a couple of our female officers went shopping and bought a few things for you since we couldn't go to your house, obviously. By the way, we have an underground entrance that is impossible to locate if you were wondering how they got the clothes here. And as for the way you came in, that is no longer in sight. You both have your own bathrooms in there as well. You'll find tooth brushes, toothpaste, soap, shampoo, conditioner; everything you need to feel more at home. Now, I have to go to back to my office and take care of some things. I'll be back to check on you both in a little while." He hugged me and apologized for all that was happening, nodded at Athena then walked down the hallway back to his office. Athena and I checked out each other's rooms and bathrooms. The clothes and shoes that were picked out for her were nice and casual and fit her perfectly. It wasn't until we were showered and settled in our beds that Athena realized her phone was disconnected. I noticed Jax brought my purse with my phone inside of it, also disconnected. I'm sure he made that happen.

CHAPTER 12

The next morning, the scent of cinnamon and coffee filled my nostrils. I opened one eye and had almost forgotten where I was. Oh yeah, the underground Star Trek. Remembering that I was stuck here, I decided to go back to sleep and hope to wake up in my own bed. My stomach growled in protest as the cinnamon aroma grew stronger. "Ugh!" I shouted to the empty room. I got out of bed, slipped on my slippers and headed out the door. I went to Athena's room, but she was already up and out. I walked down the hall to the kitchen and there she was sitting at the table shoveling a cinnamon roll down her throat.

"Good morning!" she muffled. After she finished swallowing she said, "You have got to try these cinnamon rolls! They are beyond amazing! This icing is heavenly!"

I walked over to the counter and fixed a cup of coffee. I grabbed a small plate and grabbed a warm cinnamon roll from the tray to place it on. Taking my seat I asked, "How'd you sleep?"

"Like a rock! That bed is way better than mine at home! I may move in here!" she answered.

"I slept ok. I just hated waking up and not being in my own bed."

"Quit your belly aching. Things could be a lot worse, you know."

"Yes, it could. I'm glad it's not."

"At least you have your brother here with you."

I looked at her more closely now. She's right! I do have my brother! Once again, I understood why she was so evil when we first met. I don't remember her even talking about her family. I only know she has a brother because he's playing for her in the competition. The competition! Oh no! We may miss the competition! Like she said, things could be worse.

"I am so sorry, Athena. I can't imagine how you must feel right now." She waved me off and continued eating her cinnamon roll.

I forked a bit of mine. "Mmmmm! This really is good! Oh my!" I said through a mouthful. I felt the icing build up in the corner of my mouth so I licked at it instead of using a napkin. I was not planning on letting that go to waste on a napkin!

Jax came into the kitchen. Gathering a cup of coffee, a plate of eggs, bacon, waffles with fresh strawberries and honey, he sat down, quickly graced his food then dug in. I was glad to see he still prayed. Athena and I just stared at him. He didn't even respond to our "good morning" after he walked in. After a few moments of eating, he looked up from his plate as if he just noticed us sitting there.

"What?" he asked through stuffed cheeks.

"Um, good morning?" I said this in the form of a question so he would understand that he omitted that upon entrance.

"Hungry much?" Athena said sarcastically.

"Oh! My bad! I am starving this morning! I hadn't really had a chance to eat yesterday." He finished eating just as fast as he fixed his plate. He drank his coffee, sat back in his chair and released a loud manly burp.

"Whew! Excuse me ladies. That was delicious!" Athena and I let him know how gross he was but laughed anyway. He stood up and took his plate over to the sink. He grabbed a plate and a cinnamon roll and sat back down.

"So about this money laundering case. There is a spa about a mile from Grace Temple that secretly runs an escort service." He uses air quotes at the word "secretly". "The records show that there is a lot of money being made in there but not being reported. We also found out that they hire money mules to launder their money for them."

"Mules? You mean they are using animals to hide their money? That doesn't even make sense!" I say. Jax just drops his head trying to hide a laugh. I open my palms and shrug with a 'what' look.

"A money mule in money laundering terms is a person who transfers or moves illegally acquired money on behalf of someone else, i.e. the launderer. They transfer funds in person, through a courier service, or electronically. They are also called smurfers."

"Are they little and blue too?" jokes Athena, poking me in the arm with her elbow. We both laugh.

"Funny." Jax says but he wasn't laughing. "Listen, I'm going to need to be away for a while. You'll both be in good hands here. If you need anything, just let Roxanne know, I'll introduce you to her momentarily."

"Are you sure you can't get someone else to go? This all sounds so risky! What if you don't come back? What if you get hurt? What if-?"

"Oh shut up Joy! This ain't his first rodeo! Weren't you listening when he told us he brought down a crime boss? Do you know how dangerous they are? The connections they have? He shut all of that down! I can't even believe how much of a baby you are being right now! Where's that praying worshipper?" Athena said while dramatically playing out her words.

"You shut up! I'm not being a baby! I am just looking out for my brother! Did you forget where we escaped from?" I jumped up and stood my ground at her.

"How can I forget? You bring it up every chance you get! You think you're so much better than everyone else! We all can't be God's favorite like you are! We all can't have the perfect family life like you! We all can't be the best singer/songwriter like you! God forbid if little Miss Perfect has to go through anything! Guess what Joy; you and your little family are not as perfect as you may think! You know what? At this point I'd rather be with the kidnappers than to be stuck here with you!" she yelled, and stormed out of the kitchen.

Jax yelled after her to come back, but she did not listen.

CHAPTER 13

I sat back down in my chair, stunned and furious at the same time. What did she mean by saying all of that? What does she know about my family? Do I really act the way she says? Of course not! If she knew me so well she would know where I've come from and how hard I've worked to get where I am!

"What does she know about our family?" I say this out loud not really to anyone nor was I expecting an answer. Jax sits down at the table next to me and sighs heavily.

"I guess now is as good a time as any to tell you this, Joy." He said.

"Tell me what?" He looks me in the eye, then drops his head and sighs heavily again.

"You know how I keep putting off talking to dad?"

"Yeah."

He swipes his face downward with his palm. "The day I left for Florida I stopped at the shoe store to grab a pair of sneakers for the trip. While I was headed down the men's size 12 aisle, I overheard this young lady in the next aisle over talking on the phone. I didn't really pay attention to what she was saying because it was none of my business. But then I heard her say something like, 'You're always at that church! You never have time for me, daddy!' and I thought to myself, *welcome to the club little lady!* Anyway, I went on about my business looking for shoes. Next thing I knew she switched her phone to speaker. Then I heard his voice. Of course I was like *this can't be him!* So I casually walked over to the aisle she was in. She had the phone lying on the seat next to her while she was trying on a pair of shoes. I looked down at the phone and saw his picture staring back at me!" Tears began to well up in his eyes now. "Joy! I saw our father's face on this girl's phone! She called him daddy!" He covered his face with both hands to stifle the angry cry. I couldn't believe what I was hearing!

"Jax, that's not possible! Daddy would ne-"

"Stop it Joy! You've been sheltered and always going for the safe life! You always shut out conflict or anything you didn't want to deal with! How can you even sit there and say what *daddy* would never do when he did the same thing to you! You of all people should know what he's capable of!"

And there it was. The memories of my father molesting me came flooding back to mind drowning me in fear and disgust all over again. All I could do was just sit and stare. No tears came. No anger rose. Bile violated my stomach and threatened to erupt something fierce. I tried to swallow it down, but I was failing fast. I ran to the sink and released. Afterwards, I washed my face and mouth. I sank to the floor leaning my back up against the cabinet door.

"He made me feel sorry for him." I began. "He said mom was getting too old to be the wife he needed her to be in that way. He said he didn't want to go to anyone else because that would be more of a sin in God's eyes than coming to me. He said I was the only one that could help him be a better father and Pastor. I didn't understand any of it, but I wanted our dad to be happy and do a good job. I wanted him to let you play football and go to college. He started out coming to my room laying next to me and telling me stories in the bible about how the young girls had to give themselves to their fathers and/or male siblings. 'It was how God designed it' he would say. While telling the stories, he would put my hand inside his pants and tell me to hold his penis gently and to only squeeze it when he told me to. Laying his hand on top of mine, he would rub it against him. Slow at first, then faster and more intense. He would grab my hand tighter and tell me to squeeze as he moved faster in an up and down motion. Then his body would jerk and a deep throaty sound would come out of his mouth. He'd release my hand and tell me to go wash it. I would go back to my room and wonder what just happened and why did it feel so wrong if he said it was right? But he was my father, my daddy, my protector. He can't be wrong. A few nights later he changed his pattern and began touching me down there, asking me if I liked it. When I would say no, he would remind that God would want me to like it. I still didn't like it but I was afraid to tell him that. The fear grew more intense when he decided he wanted me to feel him against me. He made me turn my back to him while he rubbed against the outside of my entrance. I think he liked this way better because he started coming in my room more often to do it that way. One night it actually slid inside me and he quickly covered my mouth before I could scream. I felt a strong pang of hate towards him that night. I went from feeling sorry, to feeling fear, and finally to feeling hatred. He kept shushing me and soothing me like a baby to make me relax. He never let himself go inside of me though. I knew then that our father was a phony and a fraud. I felt so robbed and so used after that night. He tried to do it again the next night, but I stopped him this time. I told him if he came near me again, I was going to tell mom and the church. He just stared at me and damned me to hell. Saying that the devil has gotten to me and I allowed myself to be tainted. He called me a whore. Can you believe that? He called me a whore! And this is why I am having reservations about going into that spa, Jax!" He joined me on the floor and gathered me in his arms.

"Listen sis, I am truly sorry for talking to you the way I did. I had no idea it had gotten that far with him. I would see him come out of your room sometimes fastening his belt. At first I thought you got in trouble for something, but when I seen it a second time I went to mom about it. She brushed me off and told me to stop telling lies. I was so focused on getting out of that house I didn't even try to rescue you. I guess since you didn't say anything about it, nothing was going on so I left it alone. I really am sorry! I am proud of you for picking your life up and giving over to God. I see now why this whole forgiveness thing means so much to you."

"I haven't talked to him about it since then. He hasn't talked to me about either. After you left he started taking care of me like an actual daughter. He made sure I had everything I needed and wanted, supported all my musical goals, spoiled mom out of this world. I guess for him that was his way of apologizing to both of us. One evening I came home from graduation rehearsal and he was in their bedroom on his knees with his hands raised and head thrown back crying out to God thanking Him for sparing his life and for forgiving his sins. I didn't want to disturb that so I crept back down the hall and up the stairs to my room. I thanked God for touching his soul. I didn't know then that it was more to his cries than just what he had done to me, he lied to me about not going to someone else because it would be a greater sin! She was already born! What is she, three years younger than me?"

"A year actually." Jax said. All we could do was laugh.

"All this time you kept his secret. Why?" I asked Jax

"Well my dear sister, I didn't want to hurt you and mom. Turns out mom already knew. She knew from day one. They kept it quiet for "church" reasons. You know the deal."

"Wait, Athena knows too doesn't she? That's why she's been acting so mean to me!"

"I believe she knows about you and mom. I think she just found out about me yesterday."

CHAPTER 14

Jax and I hear a noise coming from the doorway of the kitchen. We look over to see Athena standing there watching us.

"Sorry to interrupt," she said in an apologetic tone. "I couldn't help but over hear your conversation."

"How much did you hear?" I asked

"I heard everything after Jax's second deep sigh. I didn't get very far after storming off before I realized that was not the time for me to have a meltdown. I turned around to come back and heard Jax begin speaking about how he found out who I was."

"It's all pretty crazy, huh?" I said.

"Oh yeah! Look, Joy, I had no idea...I am so sorry..."

"Hey, don't give it a second thought." I interrupted. "We've all had our issues with *our* father. Now it's up to us how we handle each other. What do you say to us letting go and letting God begin the healing process?"

"I think that would be a great idea. Besides, we've gotten along so well this far why stop now?" We laugh and embrace each other in acceptance.

"Welcome to the family, Athena." Jax said. "Now let's go to the arcade so I can whip y'all in skee-ball before I leave out of here in the morning!"

~~~~~~

"Dear Jesus,
~~~~~~

Thank you for your hand of protection over us this past week. The things you have carried us through has given us strength, confidence, and trust in you. Thank you for your healing power over my family and Athena's too. Please let Ryan know that I am safe and under your protection. Give him peace of mind while he sleeps. Please keep Jax in your arms as he takes on this dangerous task to uphold justice. And Lord, thank you so much for my sister. Amen"

I finish my prayer and snuggle comfortably in my bed when I hear a soft knock at the door.

"Joy? Are you sleeping?" Athena's voice comes through the closed door in a low childlike tone. I call back for her to come in.

She comes in and takes a seat on the bed next to me.

"Can I ask you something?"

"What is it?"

"Why did you lie to Jax?"

"Lie about what?"

"I heard you tell him that your father never let himself go inside of you, but he told my mother he had to take you to the clinic for an abortion. He told her you were sneaking around with a boy and got pregnant. It wasn't until I heard your story out there to Jax that I put it all together. It was his baby, wasn't it? He also told my mother that your mother didn't know about it and that it would kill her if she did because she thought you were so innocent."

I couldn't believe what I was hearing! I sat up in the bed and tried to clear the lump in my throat.

"Wow! Sounds like your mother and our father had a pretty good relationship. I don't ever remember him saying as much as a hello to my mother in passing. I would hear them trying to stifle arguments in their bedroom." I took a deep breath before I continued. "I didn't even know I was pregnant. It was my father that brought it to my attention. He said he heard me throwing up one morning while my mother was in their bathroom taking a shower. When I came downstairs for breakfast he stared at my face and said I looked terrible. I told him I didn't feel well. The next day he came to my room with a pregnancy test telling me to go into the bathroom and use it. "Read the instructions", he said. I did just that and the stick showed two lines. I was pregnant. Next thing I know he's carting me off to the clinic where they confirmed my pregnancy. The room they examined me in is the same room they used to make me not pregnant again. You have no idea how hard it was to finally forgive him and free myself of it all. Talking it all out now let's me know I was never truly healed. Sure, I forgave him; I just didn't realize I hadn't forgiven myself." Athena scooted closer to me and put her arm around me.

"You are the bravest person I have ever met. You have got to stop protecting yourself from yourself and let God do it. It's ok to hurt and be angry, just don't beat yourself up in the process. I truly am sorry for everything I have ever said to you. I am sorry for your relationship with your-our father. Everything is going to work out fine."

"At first I thought you came in here to rub it in my face and point out once again how imperfect I am. Thank you for helping me see me the way God does."

"And for the record my mother and our father may have gotten along well, which was only for my sake, but my mother was on to him. She saw right through him. She tried to get me to befriend you years ago, but I wouldn't do it because I was jealous of you. I saw the lifestyle you had and how our dad was always with you and hardly ever with me. I really wanted to ruin you and scratch your eyes out. But God had a different plan. He didn't want us to be like our earthly father, He wanted us to be like Him!"

"That is so true. Let me be the one to tell Jax, ok?"

"Of course, Sis. This is not my story to tell anyone."

CHAPTER 15

"Oh man! This Philly cheese steak breakfast sandwich is everything right now!" I said through stuffed cheeks. Athena is filling her cheeks as well and nodding her head in agreement. "Mmm! It really is! I can't get over how tender the meat is, the egg is fluffy and buttery, and the croissant is toasted just right!" she mumbled between chews.

Today was the first day Athena and I actually got to see the chef. He is clean and rugged looking at the same time. From what I could tell around his apron, his body is lean, and his arms are thick and solid, not muscular though. He is about 6' tall, tanned skin, dark brown eyes and hair. His face is fairly attractive and clean with deep perfectly rounded dimples in his cheeks. Every time he smiled, his whole body seemed to smile with him. I could tell and taste that he loved his job.

As we grab breakfast sandwich number two from the platter placed in front of us, Jax walks in with a short stocky woman.

"Good morning, ladies! This is Roxanne. She'll be here to make sure you have everything you need while I'm gone."

"You mean she'll be here to babysit us!" Athena said sarcastically.

"It's not like that, Athena. Listen, I told you both before, it's not safe for you to go out anywhere right now. Roxanne will make sure you are very well taken care of."

"I totally respect that you ladies are adults. I am simply here to make sure you are safe and comfortable. I'm not here to tell you to clean your room and brush your teeth." She said this in a joking yet militant tone.

After breakfast, Jax asks me and Athena to follow him. He takes us back through his office and codes another white board.

We look at each other and shrug our shoulders wondering what he is up to this time. The white board slides open to the right. Jax steps through the door and turns to look at us as if to say 'come on'. We step through the door and my eyes take in the most breathtaking sight! I think this room trumps the library!

"It's a music room!" Athena says in excitement.

"Jax, when did you do this? How did you do this? You got a keyboard with a drum pad, a Guitar and two mics! These monitor speakers are amazing!" I said striking a few jazz chords on the keys. "How long do you plan on us being here?" I asked.

"Don't worry it's just temporary. I just want to help make your time here comfortable and enjoyable. I figured you both would like this most of all."

"Most definitely!" we said in unison.

"The acoustics in this room is all that!" Athena said. She walked over to one of the microphones and started singing. Man her voice is beautiful! I went to the keyboard and followed her flow.

I glanced over at Jax. His eyes were huge in amazement. I am so in awe at how beautiful and clean her voice is! The runs she renders roll from her throat like melting butter! Her vocal style reminds me of a mix between Lauren Hill and Faith Evans when she goes from low to high effortlessly! When she jazzes out her last lyric, Jax applauds with tears in his eyes.

"You ladies sound wonderful together. Joy, I was mesmerized by your true heart worship song during the service that Sunday and now this? Girl, I didn't know you had gotten so good on the keyboard! And Athena, your voice is everything!"

"Jax, are you crying?" I asked with a mock smile.

"Hey, when it comes to good music I don't mind being in my feelings! I'm serious you both have beautiful voices and Joy, you have mad music skills. Y'all could, no, should put a hurt on the masses!"

"Joy and I come from two different worlds. I'm really not about that church life. That is the one place I do not trust anyone nor do I want to try. Joy is a true worshipper. It's in her blood. She couldn't get away from it even if she tried."

Wow, if Athena only knew the power of her voice. If she could only get past whatever is making her feel the way she feels about church and understand that it should not determine whether or not to have a covenant with God, she *could* put a hurting on the masses. Now I understand her questioning my faith before. Looks like I need to be a better example around her.

CHAPTER 16

Later that night, Jax left out on his mission. I'm still trying to get over the fact that he is an FBI agent. After a hot shower and putting on my new pj's Roxanne went out and got for me along with other items Athena and I put on a list, I decided to go into the entertainment room to find something on TV that would ease my mind of everything. Maybe watch a comedy or something. I settled on an old black and white film starring Cary Grant. He is my all time favorite actor from that era.

"Joy! Joy! Wake up!"

"Hmmm!" I groaned. Athena is shaking me like she was demonstrating how an earthquake works.

"Wake up! I have to talk to you!"

I tried to sit up and focus my life in the land of the living but felt a sharp gripping pain in my neck and shoulder. I could barely lift my head. I must've gotten extremely comfy after that shower and movie. I do not remember falling asleep on this couch.

"Ouch! My head and neck is stuck!"

"Here, let me help you!" Athena said, and grabbed me by my head and yanked me up in a sitting position. I yelped.

"Dang girl! Go ahead and take my head off my shoulders, why don't you?"

"I need you to focus on what I am about to tell you!"

"What is it? What's going on?"

"It's that Roxanne chick! There's something about her that does not sit right!"

"What are you talking about?"

"I went into my bathroom to start the shower. I like to let it run a few minutes before getting in to make sure it's hot enough. I was heading to my room to get my head wrap to protect my hair from the shower cap, when I saw her in the mirror going through my drawers!"

"What? Why would she do that?"

"I don't know! After she left out, I followed her to her room and overheard her get on the phone telling someone it wasn't in there, and that she would check the other room!"

"What other room?"

"How am I supposed to know? There's quite a few around here!"

"Athena, it could've been Jax asking her to look for something that might've been left in there before we got here!"

"What if it wasn't? I'm telling you there's something about that Tangina looking woman I don't like!" I had to laugh at her referencing Roxanne to the short spirit chaser from the Poltergeist movie.

"I think your trust issues are getting the better of you, girl!"

"Whatever! I'm not going to stop looking over my shoulder while I'm here!"

"Let's just go to bed, I'm sure she had a legitimate reason for being in your room. Just ask her about it at breakfast!"

"After that dinner we had, I don't know if I'm going to have breakfast!"

"Yeah, that chef did his thang again in that kitchen!"

One thing I hate is getting up to use the bathroom in the middle of the night from a deep sleep. I'm not a fan of getting up to write a song either, but I don't hate it. I try lying here as long as I can hoping the urge will go away and find an open spot in my bladder to sit in for another four hours. After about two minutes, I learn that it did not. I yank the covers off of me and notice how extremely cold it is. What in the world? I sit up and get out of bed to go to the bathroom. Something is totally not right here. But before I go exploring, I am going to the bathroom this time. As I finish relieving myself, I feel the room jerk. Ok, now I know something isn't right! I hurry and wash my hands and leave the bath room. Before I make it to the door, I get knocked down by a second jerk of the room. I scramble to my feet and make it to the door. It's locked! What is going on! "Hey!!" I yell and bang on the door as hard as I can! "Athena? Are you out there? Can you hear me?" I run over to the wall that we shared and bang on it. "Athena? Are you there?" I press my ear to the wall hoping to hear her voice.

"Joy! Joy the door is locked! The room keeps jerking! What is going on?" I can hear the fear and anger in her voice which gets clearer showing a sign that she is walking closer to the wall.

"I don't know, Athena!"

"I bet this is Roxanne's doing! I told you I didn't trust her!"

"We don't know that for sure! Maybe there's a tornado happening!"

"Did you forget we are underground you goober?"

"Oh yeah! Groundhogs?"

"Oh, better yet, Bugs Bunny!!" she yells sarcastically.

"You don't have to be so mean about it! I was just trying to make it sound less scary!"

"Just stop, okay?"

The room jerked once more. We screamed from the impact.

"Athena, are you ok?" I asked the wall. She didn't answer.

"Athena? Athena? Are you there! Say something!"

The bedroom door flung open and she quickly stepped inside.

"Dorothy, we are not in Kansas anymore!"

CHAPTER 17

"What do you mean by that?" I asked with a shiver in my voice.

"I mean, somehow we have been disjoined from our hidden quarters!"

"Are you serious?"

"Listen, we need to find a way out of here and figure out what's going on! Jax isn't here to help us this time. We are going to have to save ourselves, Joy! I need you to man up and put your big girl panties on right now!"

"Ok! Let's do this Sis! If I can survive excessive chloroform, I can survive whatever's beyond that door!" Under my breath I say "I hope" and ask God to please let me be right and strong.

Athena slowly opened the door and looked out. She turned to me and put her index finger to her lips, then waved for me to follow her out the door. We stepped into the dim lit hallway. Instead of the entertainment room being in front of us, there was a plain ivory wall. The hallway only went one direction and that was to the left coming out of our door.

"Welp, let's do this!" Athena said. I followed her down the hallway. It wasn't as long as the one where we were staying, so we made it to the end in just a few short steps.

"You ready to see what's behind the door?" Athena asked. I nodded. She opened the door. There is another hallway, a longer one with a window that followed it. We stopped to look through the window. It revealed that we were higher up than we expected to be. Below us is a brightly lit large warehouse. There are hundreds of small rectangle tables and chairs at each one lined up like a class room. Each table has a sewing machine attached to it. We look at each other in wonder and continue walking along the window staring down into the warehouse. Athena stops abruptly.

"Look!" she whispers loudly. I look in the direction of her pointing finger and see more tables and sewing machines. Only this set has women sitting at them working. They looked to be no older than thirty.

"Factory workers?" I say this meaning it to be a statement, but it sounds like a question.

"Yes, but it doesn't look like they get paid to be here! Look at their ankles! They are wearing chains that are linked to the table legs and the table legs are bolted to the floor!"

"Oh my goodness! They're prisoners!"

Just as I say that, a door opens in the corner of the warehouse and at least twelve more women around the same age are forced inside wearing knee length faded blue house dresses and shackles.

"Those poor women are products of human trafficking!"

"Athena, do you think that's why we're here? Who brought us here? How did they get us here?"

"Well I don't think they got us here be sewing teachers that's for sure."

"What are we going to do now?"

"C'mon!"

We found another door but listened at it before opening it. Slowly turning the handle, Athena peeked inside. She widened the entrance and we pushed our way through. There are staircases going up.

"Maybe we can make our way out of here! We already know we're underground, if we keep going up, we may find our way out of here!" She said.

Unfortunately, we have reached the last set of stairs. No chance of going up and out from here. Going through yet another door, we find ourselves facing another window. This room had about ten women in it! They all looked under the age of twenty-five and dressed as if they were going out for a night on the town! But they didn't look like they were excited about it.

"Joy, I wonder if these are the women they use for the escort service Jax told us about?"

"It seriously looks like it!"

"Joy, all of these women here are missing from their families and friends! Their normal lives have come to an end here! They are forever slaves to whoever is running this operation!"

"I know! I think they mean for us to join them! The question is, which of them are they going to make us join?"

"That's a very good question my dear!" This response did not come from Athena. We turned to look behind us.

"Chef?" Athena and I say at the same time.

"What are you doing here?" We ask.

He pulls out a gun and demands us to turn around and walk in front of him.

"I advise you both to cooperate and don't do anything stupid." He said

CHAPTER 18

The Chef forces us down a corridor with blue lights along the sides of the floor. These were the only lights glowing to lead us along.

"Turn left at the end." He instructed.

We turned left and ran smack dab into a door.

"Open it!" he ordered.

Athena turned the knob and pushed open the door.

The room is cold and grey with a dim white light in the ceiling. The Chef pulls out his cell phone, pushes a button, holds it up to his ear and says, "They're here," then leaves out the door locking it behind him.

"Let me guess, you thought you were escaping this place, huh?" Athena and I whirled around to see where the voice was coming from. Further into the room sat four females on a black leather couch.

"What?" Athena said.

"If you're brought to this room that means you were caught trying to escape or you were simply caught. They have cameras everywhere, and I do mean everywhere." another one said with a thick British accent.

"Yep, even in the bathrooms." The third one piped in

"How old are you?" asked the fourth one.

Athena looked at the second one and asked just how many times she tried to escape to know what that room was for.

"None." she answered. "I'm the preparer."

"How can you tell which we are?" I asked.

"Cameras, Joy! What, exactly do you prepare?" Athena asked

"I-we," she gestures a hand towards the other three women, "prepare you for your new job. I'm Mara; this is Corinne, Judi, and Brenda. You see, you were chosen to be our new business women. You already have the looks and the shapely bodies; we just need to make sure you have the attitude and the fashion to carry it out."

Athena looked at me and I widened my eyes at her. She stiffened her lips together signaling me not to say anything about what we knew concerning the escort service.

"You both look to be about 32, correct?" This question came from Brenda who looked to be the youngest of the four. She had reddish brown hair that look amazing against her clear light brown skin.

"I'm 31, my sister is 32." Athena said. "Why, does that matter?"

"It helps us to place you with the right job, that's all." said Corinne. I had to stifle a laugh at the sound of her mousy voice. Her looks and all reminded me of Audrey from the movie Little Shop of Horrors.

"Let's go ladies; they aren't going to wait on us all day!"

"Hold your horses, Judi! They'll wait if they want things done right!" Mara said.

"What happens if we refuse our jobs?" asked Athena.

"You get tortured or killed." Mara said, as if Athena was only asking what the weather was.

Mara walked over to a mirrored wall and slid it open from the middle. She led us into another room that was set up like a huge dressing room. There were clothes, vanity tables loaded with make-up, toiletries, and jewelry of every kind. There were three full bathrooms without doors. Talk about not having any privacy!

Mara and Brenda took care of preparing our outward appearance while Judi and Corinne educated us on how to be 'ladies of the evening', according to the jobs that awaited us. My heart pounded at the thought of being taken by a total stranger and not being able to do anything about it, unless I wanted to die of course. This cannot be happening! We have got to do something! There has to be a way out of this mess!

After they adorned us to their liking, we were led to the same room where we saw the other ladies dressed as we were.

"You will have a seat in here until you are selected. Remember, once you are selected, you will do whatever you are told to do, act however you are instructed to act, and speak only if spoken to." Mara said, then turned on her heels and walked away.

"Joy, we have got to do something! Not just for you and I, but for all these women!"

"I know! At first I was thinking any moment now Jax is going to pop up and get us out of here like he did the last time we escaped!"

"Yeah, that would be great! Humph, first we made our escape to Jax, now we have made a fast escape to hell! How long do you think we'll have to do this? What if this is it for us? Joy, I am not equipped to be anybody's professional escort!"

Before I could even respond to Athena, the door opened and the Chef came in and directed two of the women to come with him.

"Athena," I immediately try to encourage her soon as he leaves the room. "We have to be strong! We have to keep our eyes and ears open! There has to be a way out of here and around those cameras! I'm going to find it! I'm beginning to think this is *NOT* part of the escort service Jax told us about! I think this is much bigger! I can't imagine he even knows about this place! The operation he told us about explains how all parties involved were willing to be a part of it. These women are scared and clueless!" The women around us were indeed quiet and visibly scared, although warned not to cry so as to not ruin their makeup and to keep a positive look on their faces, I'm sure. They weren't the least bit interested in me and Athena's presence.

"I am totally convinced that Roxanne and the Chef are in this together! I have been trying to figure out why, but it's a crazy mystery to me right now!" Athena said.

"At this point, I am deemed to agree with you! In any case, we have got to find a way out of this!"

CHAPTER 19

"You two, let's go!" The Chef has returned to take us to our doom. I wonder where we go after the job is over? The other two ladies never came back. Where are they? I grab Athena's hand tight as we walk towards the door. He leads us to a lobby where Mara is standing and waiting. The sight of the outside takes me by surprise and I gasp.

Joy leans over to me and whispers, "You think we can make a break for it?"

"If you're thinking of running off once outside, I suggest you get the thought right out of your head my beauties. There will be guns focused on you to the car and another car will be following us to our destination. Not to mention our chauffeur is trained to shoot now and ask questions later. Also, while you are working we will be right outside waiting for you to return to the car." Mara says with a mocking grin on her face. I just want to slap it off! Isn't it funny how someone can be so nice and so mean at the same time?

We pull up to a fancy looking no name hotel that has a private entrance. Mara steps out of the car and instructs us to do the same. There are men standing outside of the car behind us with their hands inside their suit jacket breast pockets letting us know they are prepared to take us out if need be. Once inside, Mara picks up the phone receiver from a phone hanging on the wall next to the door. "Hello, Mr. Clayton. I have two employees here to service your room for you. Is it ok to send them up now?"

She nods her head and say a couple of uh-huh's then hangs up the phone. She instructs us toward the elevator, making sure to stay close behind us. There is only one indicator button to push. When the doors open we step inside and she pushes the button, the only button, marked "PH". The elevator dings and the doors open.

"You will go through the left door, and you will take the right door," Mara directed Athena to the left and me to the right. We exchanged horrified glances. This is the moment!

"Remember your stance, posture, and conduct. Any hint of dissatisfaction will have consequences. Because our clients demand utmost privacy, I cannot linger here. I will meet you at the entrance downstairs where we came in."

"Ok Lord, we need you so bad right now! Please make a way for Athena and me to keep ourselves!" I prayed as I entered the room.

"Come on in young lady," he said. "Relax a while."

"Um, ok." That was all I could muster. I was trembling so bad I didn't want to talk and ruin my rapport.

"Don't worry; I don't want you to talk to me at all. Just do everything I tell you, and we will get along just fine."

I smile and swallow the lump that has lodged itself in my throat.

He guides me to a plush chair placed in front of his bed. "Have a seat my dear." he said.

"Now take off your shoes, unbutton the top four buttons of your shirt, and relax your arms on the arms of the chair. Oh, and pull your skirt to mid thigh and cross your legs."

I am trying my hardest not to show my shaking hands as I unbutton my shirt. My heart is pounding so fast I feel like it is going to shoot out of my mouth! When I finish following his instructions, I just relax in the chair and stare at him, trying to paste a smile on my face.

"You're doing just fine young lady, just fine! Oh yeah!" He takes off his shirt and undoes his pants. I'm really hoping he does not want to violate my mouth!

He lies on the bed, grabs a remote control and points it over my head. What is he up to? I look up waiting for an object to come out of the ceiling or something but it doesn't. A TV comes on. So I'm just going to sit here and watch you watch television? This is getting pretty weird! He pushes a couple of buttons, and then relaxes back on his pillows. He takes his pants off and begins to rub himself through his underwear! What is happening?

"Don't move!" he says with more firmness in his voice this time. If he's not going to touch me, you can best believe I will not move a single muscle!

He turns the television up louder. I hear a man's groan and wet sounds. He turns the television up even louder. The man's voice on the TV is giving instructions to someone, but they aren't vocally responding. The sounds get more intense and I realize the man on the bed in front of me is fully naked and pleasing himself!

"Watch me!" he said. "Watch how I do what I do!"

Seriously? I'm not complaining, grossed out, but not complaining! As I continue to watch, I notice there is something familiar about him. He reaches over the side of the bed and opens the drawer of the nightstand and pulls out a woman's wig. What is happening in this room right now! He then reaches over the side of the bed again and pulls out a dummy doll from underneath! He puts the wig on, and then positions the doll's mouth, which is a male doll by the way, to sing in his microphone.

That's it! I know where I have seen this man before! While he's handling his business, I carefully take a peek at the screen on the wall above my head. My stomach lurches to my throat and I force it back down. This is too much! Too crazy! There are two men lying in the bed on the television screen; Elder Trevor Stanton and Pastor Ronald Spencer, together, entangled in a fury of sexual pleasure! I hurry to regain my stance in the chair and try to steady my breathing and choke down an outcry. The person on the bed in front of me is not only the *woman* I saw giving Elder Trevor a mean stare that Sunday at the church just before I went into the prayer room, she is also the *man* that I saw with Trevor in the Pastor's office! At that time, he wore that wig and full blown make up and women's clothing! I thought he *was* a woman until I saw Trevor on his knees in front of him doing the same thing that he is making this doll do to him right now!

"Ok young lady, here comes the finale! I am going to look you in the eye when it happens so you'd better be watching!" He rose up, flipped the doll on its back with its head facing my direction, pushed its legs over its shoulders, and plowed into its anal entry over and over. He stared at the screen plowing more intensely as the action grew. Then he looked me straight in the eyes and said, "Watch this!" He gave the doll a hard thrust and let himself go inside of it. He gave one more thrust and screamed, "Watch!" I saw some of his liquid spew out of the doll's mouth. Ok, that was gross!

After letting out one more scream, he passed out. I thought he was dead until I heard him snore. I stood up to take a look at the screen. They were sleeping as well. Just as I was about to grab my shoes, I saw a female figure tiptoe across the TV screen. Athena!

CHAPTER 20

"I cannot believe that I had to sit there and watch your Pastor and that Elder from your church go at it! They literally made me sit there with my shirt partly unbuttoned, shoes off, and legs crossed in a chair with my arms resting on the arms of the chair and watch them go at it like hungry dogs!"

"Yeah, well I went through the same thing with a transgender, only he was doing a dummy doll while watching my Pastor and Elder Trevor going at it on his television screen!"

"What? How?"

"He must have that room bugged with cameras or something! The chair he had me seated in sits directly under the wall where the TV was mounted. While he was in his bliss I stole glances! And that's not all! I was reminded of what I saw when I peeked in the Pastor's study! That guy in there was making Trevor hum tunes to his manhood, only he was dressed as a she!"

"What is happening in that church?"

"The Bible is playing itself out, Sis! Jesus could come any minute and so many 'church folk' are going to miss Him!"

"Well, I wish He would come right now so we can get out of here!"

"How are we going to get out of here? They're waiting for us out there!"

"We better figure something out quick before those three wake up!"

"Joy, look over there! A laundry elevator! It looks big enough for both of us! C'mon! Hurry up!"

"I'm coming!"

When got to the laundry elevator, we noticed there were no buttons to push to open it.

"What do we do now?" Athena asked.

"Hold on, I'm looking!" I feel around the wall of the elevator for a hidden push panel or something.

"Joy! Look!" Athena is gesturing toward the ground in front of the elevator. A foot pedal, similar to the type used to open a trash can, was pressed against it. I step on it and the door turns in a circular motion until an opening reveals itself in front of us.

The laundry elevator takes us down to the basement of the hotel. Along with all the sheets and towels down here, there are maid uniforms, shoes, and head scarves.

"Are you thinking what I'm thinking?" I ask Athena.

"Yes, let's do it!"

As we dress ourselves in the maid uniforms and try to work out an escape plan, I throw in words of prayer and thankfulness to God that even though we were forced to watch the inappropriate acts of those three men, He made the way for us to still keep ourselves!

"You know," Athena begins, "I have to say that after all we have been through up to this point I am starting to see the difference between God and Church. Every time you prayed or mentioned Him, He's been faithful and present. How amazing is it that he caused them to fall into a deep sleep to give us the chance to get out of there! I get why they say the building doesn't make the Church, the people do. We are the Church. We are supposed to be the physicians. There are so many people that need healing, salvation, and help. I see now that all these sufferings are a product of the sacrifice Jesus made for us on the Cross. Joy, we have got to do something to help all of those women get out of that place!"

"We definitely will, Sis! I noticed you said "we" about who we are as the Church. Does this mean you are willing to give it another shot?"

"All I'm saying is that there are a lot of people in need of the life benefits of Jesus Christ. When it comes to the 'church folk' so to speak, no thanks! Now, let's get moving!"

She crosses in front of me to grab a scarf. I smile at her and her softening heart.

We make our way out of the laundry area and into the hallway. We find the door to the housekeeping staff's quarters and walk in. Keeping our heads down we try to quickly make our way to the door but a tall thin no nonsense man points at us and instructs us to come to him. We look at each other wide eyed hoping he didn't ask us to remove our scarves from our faces.

"I haven't got all day! Come quickly and get your assignments for the evening! Good job with the face coverings, I don't need you calling off sick from the germs in those rooms!" he barked.

Without saying a word, we approach him. He hands an envelope to each one of us containing a pass key card and a schedule card with times and room numbers listed. He then pushed us aside and called out to the others to do the same. Athena and I looked at each other and moved forward towards the door. We reached the elevators, press the arrow going up, step on, and hit 'L' for lobby.

CHAPTER 21

When the elevator door opens, Mara is spotted standing by the lobby doors, pacing back and forth while talking on her phone. We quickly hide behind the hallway wall at the lobby entrance, feeling relieved by her distraction.

"They must be extremely pleased with the two new girls, I haven't gotten any phone calls of rebellion or kickback.

Yes, they will be their regulars I'm sure. Alright. Yes sir."

She hung up the phone with a pleased look on her face.

"Look! There's a side door at the end of the hallway! C'mon." Athena grabs my hand and pulls me along.

We get about ten feet from the door when we hear someone call out to us. We freeze in our tracks.

"Excuse me; can I get some towels in here?" A woman wearing only a T-shirt that barely covered her private areas stepped outside her hotel room door to wave us down.

In a very thick Spanish accent, Athena says, "So sorry miss, eh we leave for today, no? Ehm, next shift five minutes!" She pushes me along as the woman makes racial slurs and yells something about us going back to our country.

We finally make it outside and begin walking towards the road. We both sigh with relief and snatch our scarves from our faces when we get far enough away from the hotel.

"Can you tell where we are out here?" Athena asks.

"Not really. Let's see what this next street sign says."

"Man, talk about déjà vu! This time we are NOT getting in anyone's car! I don't care who it is!"

"Agreed!"

We walk about 2 miles when I realize where we are. I gasp at the knowledge that we are only one street away from my own!

"What is it, Joy?"

"Athena, the next street up is Culver!"

"So?"

"That's my street! I can't believe we are literally this close to home! This is the furthest I've ever come to this area from my house! I had no idea the back of that hotel is almost in my backyard so to speak!"

"Praise Jesus! Please tell me you have a phone there!"

"Believe it or not I do have a landline phone and all the important numbers that are in my cell phone are listed next to it!"

"Hey, I'm not judging! I'm overly thankful!"

As soon as we turn the corner onto my street, we notice all the cars parked near my house. I stop and grab Athena's arm.

"We can't go there! Look at all the cars!"

"So? What if it's Jax and his people?"

"What if it's not? You know that we can't take any chances now!"

"So what do we do?"

"C'mon, I have an idea!"

The home Jax and I grew up in was only two streets over. The back yard was and still is a wooded area. Jax and I would play back there all the time. One day we wandered a little too far from home and stumbled on an abandoned shed. At the time it was fairly sturdy and safe so we built onto it with some fallen tree branches and logs. It was our own private fort. Now that I think about it, I can see why Jax chose the FBI profession. He was so good at making or finding hiding places when we played hide-n-seek. As we got older, he said we should go there every once in a while and keep it up. He said we should add leaves and vines to it each time to make it blend in with the scenery. You never knew if or when we would need a safe haven.

I went there more often than he did, of course. Even in my adulthood, I would go a couple of times a month to make sure it was still here. The last time I went was just about a month ago, a few days before I was taken. I added a flagpole for us. I fixed it so no one would know it was there besides Jax and me. I tied a laundry line to a long thin pole from top to bottom making it into a pulley, tied a red scarf around the outside of the line, then covered both the pole and the scarf in leaves and vines. I rotated the line down then up to make the scarf rise and fall as if it was a flag. I sent a video to Jax's phone demonstrating it to him. I told him if it's raised, one of us is inside, if not it was empty.

"Joy, where are we going?"

"We're almost there!"

"Almost where?" I ignore her and focus on the path that started the way into the woods.

About a half a mile into the woods, I see the shed, which from where we're standing now looks like a log cabin covered in greenery.

"It's beautiful!" I whisper.

"What's beautiful? All I see is an old log cabin covered in vines!"

I look it over and raise my eyes to the flag pole. The scarf is lifted! It's lifted!!

"It's lifted! Athena, it's lifted!" I ran as fast as I could to the cabin.

"What's lifted?" I hear her yell from behind me.

"Just come on already!"

I burst inside and my heart leaps then melts all at once!

"Ryan! What are you doing here?" He grabs me and lifts me off the floor swinging me around.

"Joy! I thought I'd never see you again!" He looks over my shoulder and sees Athena standing there in shock. I couldn't tell if it was from seeing Ryan or the inside of the cabin, which is fabulous by the way. He walks over to her and hugs her.

"Are you ladies ok? Joy, I remembered you bringing me here once and telling me the story behind it. I was going crazy not knowing where you were or if you were alive or what! I prayed and fasted for both of you to return safe! Then it hit me that you could've escaped the kidnappers and come here to your safe haven! I ran out of places to look for you so I decided to stay here and prepare it and wait for you! I even raised the flag!"

"Ryan I am so happy you're here! Thank you for not giving up on me!"

"I would never do that!" We embraced again, longer this time.

"Oh get a room! Sheesh!" Athena said. "Ryan, have you seen or talked to my brother or my parents?"

"Yes, everyone is worried sick about you. They are doing ok, just worried of course." Athena dropped her head and moved to a chair in the corner of the cabin. Ryan had truly made this a comfortable safe haven. Except for heat and electricity, it was like a small furnished home. The furniture was used, of course, but in good shape nonetheless.

CHAPTER 22

We settled in and shared everything that had happened over the past month. When I told him about Pastor Spencer and Elder Trevor, he was dumbfounded and sorrowful for the First Lady. He said both men had been in church and participating in prayer for my return. Both were functioning in the ministry as normal. Athena did a vomiting motion in response. He mentioned how Drake was even more colorful during Praise and Worship since I wasn't there.

"So, now what do we do?" Athena asked.

"I think we should find Jax and figure out how to get those women rescued." I said. They both agreed.

"We can go to the spa where he's staking out." said Athena.

"My car is parked over on the next street. Since we don't have to go past your visitors Joy, we can all go together."

"Good idea!" I said.

Athena piped in and suggested we leave now since it's almost dark and we wouldn't risk being seen by anyone.

"I'm good with that. There is a restaurant near the spa. I can park around back and run in and grab us some food. I'll text Jax and let him know when we're there." said Ryan.

For the past two years, I have been trying to stay away from beef. Tonight I greedily welcomed it with opened mouth! It was the best burger I have ever tasted in my life! The crinkle cut fries were taking my taste buds to the stage!

Athena was eating just as hungrily as I was. Between the two of us the eating sounds were pure harmony.

Just as we finished our food, a black and gold SUV pulled up beside Ryan's car.

"Oh no, they found us!" Athena said

The window rolled down and Jax stuck his head out.

Ryan rolled his window down to hear what Jax had to say.

"Everybody get out of the car and get in with me! Hurry up!" he instructed.

We did as he said.

"Boy are we glad to see you!" I said, reaching over to hug his neck.

"Same here, sis!"

"Where are we going?"

"I'm taking y'all to a hotel and then going back to the underground headquarters to bust up that trafficking ring!"

"What about the laundering here? Aren't they connected?" Athena asked.

"No they're not. This is a small operation. As is said before, the parties involved in this one are willing parties. The one you came from is much bigger and more dangerous. This one here at the spa is already busted and taken care of."

"I figured as much from the set up and the scared women!" I said.

Athena jumps in saying, "That Roxanne is behind all of this! I'm telling you, I did not trust her for a second!"

"Actually, Roxanne figured out that the Chef was up to no good. I hid a stun gun in your top drawer months before y'all came. I sent her to your room to get it, and use it on him, but it was gone. Somehow he found it, stunned her instead, and locked her in her room. He called the leader and let them know I had gone and the 'babysitter' was taken care of. Then y'all were taken. When she regained her bearings, she was able to escape the room. She reached out to me to let me know how y'all were taken by detachment of your rooms and that she was going to find a way to save you. Thanks to the Chef, they have been building an underground operation right along with us. Since they knew the floor plan, courtesy of the Chef also, they were able to have your rooms rigged for the detachment. Roxanne allowed herself to get caught in order to get on the inside and try to find y'all. She is in the labor section of the warehouse."

"Jax I want to go with you! I want to help rescue those women!" I said

"Are you crazy? Ain't no way I'm letting you go back in there!"

"But Jax-"

"No Joy!" he cut me off.

We pulled up to the hotel and Athena immediately shouts,

"Jax! We can't stay here! This is where they think we still are! Look! Joy, there's Mara sitting in the lobby!"

"She can't possibly think we are still in there!"

"Who is Mara?" Ryan and Jax both ask in unison.

"She's the leader of the 'ladies of the night' portion of the ring!" I replied.

"The security goons are still standing around as well!" Athena said.

Jax pulled out his phone, punched in some numbers, then pulled off. As we got further down the road, we heard sirens blaring behind us.

"That problem is solved." Jax said. Ten minutes later we are pulling up at a different hotel. Parking at the door, Jax hops out and instructs us to do the same. I was the last to get out due to having to put my shoes all the way on my feet. They were tired from all the walking so I slipped out of them just enough to rest my heels on the backs of them. When I stepped out of the car, they had already reached the door. I took two steps toward them the felt something hot hit the side of my body. Everything went into slow motion. I saw Jax slowly running towards me with his eyes wide and mouth forming my name in a screaming motion. Ryan and Athena were right behind him doing the same thing. Before I hit the ground I tried to look in the direction where I'd been hit to see what it was and my eyes landed on a man holding a gun. My vision blurred then everything went black.

EPILOGUE

Six Months Later

"Who would've thought that I would be standing in this very place today? This position has been expected of me for years and I stayed away from it. I didn't want it. I told myself and God that I didn't want to be anything like my father; yet, here I am holding the baton.

I thank God for all of you for allowing me to be your new pastor and leader. I promise you I do not take this position lightly. This ministry will go beyond these four walls. We have helped bring down a dangerous human trafficking ring and will continue to do all we can to keep our community and families safe.

Witnessing my sister's life almost being taken was an eye opening experience. Sitting with her in that hospital room day and night for two weeks praying to the good Lord to please spare her life. When he answered my prayers, I knew then that He is truly real and He is definitely in control no matter what. But my faith didn't just strengthen because of my sister's healing; it strengthened because of my own healing. He fixed my heart to forgive and to be forgiven. Joy always told me that forgiveness is a powerful weapon and she is 1,000% right!" Jax looks out at our parents who are sitting in the congregation smiling and saying amens and yeses in response to his words. "I vow to spend the rest of my life living, teaching, preaching, and witnessing about the goodness of God!"

When Jax finished his testimony and exhortation to the Lord, he signaled for Praise and Worship to begin. The band had already started worshipping the CeCe Winans version of the song The Goodness of God, but I sang original lyrics that flowed in the same key:

Your love is greater than any other
Your proof is in my liberty
Your love is greater than any other
Jesus you're for me, just you for me
Your healing power takes me over
Your strength is perfect for me
Your healing power takes me over
Jesus you're for me, just you for me
When I need held you're just for me
For reassurance in my darkest hour

I turn to Athena, who is standing diagonally behind me, switch places with her, urge her to repeat the verses and continue singing the song to completion. Drake embraces me in a big bear hug and says, "Welcome back!" in my ear. Good thing I am totally healed from the gunshot wound.

The band melodically flows with Athena. Now that she has given her heart to Christ, her worship is genuine, passionate, and personal. Everyone is in worshipful tears and prayer. Once she has finished the verses; she motions for us to go into the heart of the song in harmony. The band follows bringing up the force and height:

Just Jesus, just Jesus
Just Jesus for me
Just Jesus, just Jesus
Just Jesus for me

After a couple of stances of the breakdown, she motions to bring it back down to steady worship mode and end the song:

When I need help, you're just for me
When I need strength you're just for me
In my darkest hour you're just for me
Just Jesus, Jesus for me
Just Jesus, Jesus for me

~~~~~~

Finding out about First Lady Spencer and the CEO of the Chesterfield Music School, Jane Palmer, being the leaders of the human trafficking ring brought the community in shock and mourning for weeks. I held the First Lady in such high regard, that I never even fathomed she could have any part of the human man left in her body. I was convinced that she was all spiritual inside and out. Just proves that God is the only one flawless and that no one should or nothing should be held higher than Him.

After the two women's arrests, the Pastor and Elder Trevor left the church for fear of being ridiculed if found out about their relationship. Neither Athena nor I ever told anyone what we witnessed in that hotel room, however, we continue to keep them in prayer. We were told that the Pastor had no idea about the human trafficking or his wife's involvement in it. He only found out about the private escort services through Trevor, who did not reveal his sources.
~~~~~~

The victims of the trafficking ring were released to their families and are attending counseling sessions to deal with the trauma brought to their lives. They are also current members of Grace Temple Community Church. Jax has formed an auxiliary for Human Trafficking Awareness. He arranged for an officer to attend the meetings and events every month to educate others of this profitable crime and how to stay safe in their surroundings.

After service, my parents and Ryan joined Jax and I for dinner at my house. I also invited Athena and her brother to join us. My mom helped me with the preparations, of course. We made the traditional Thanksgiving meal, even though it isn't thanksgiving. Athena offered to bring a peach cobbler and ice cream for dessert. Ryan brought the beverages.

Shortly after setting the dining room table, Athena and her brother arrived. "I'll get it!" I yelled through the house in response to the ringing doorbell. I went to the door and opened it with excitement.

"Come in, come in!"

"Hey sis!" Athena greeted me with a hug. "I want you to meet my brother. Aaron, this is my sister Joy, Joy this is your half brother Aaron."

We lock eyes for about 5 seconds before I break the silence, saying, "Aaron, it's a pleasure to meet you. Please, come in. Let me take that pie and ice cream off your hands. Athena, could you kindly open the door?" I swiftly head to the kitchen, placing the pie on the counter and the ice cream in the freezer.

Meanwhile, my mother escorts them to their seats in the dining room among the other guests.

"Joy, come sit here," Jax signals for me to take the seat between him and Ryan. With my focus on reaching my designated seat, I comply with Jax's suggestion. As I settle in, I lift my gaze and notice that I am seated directly across from the man who had put on the disgusting doll performance at the hotel the night I was shot!

THE END